MW01166483

GETTING IN
THE WIND

BY

HARLAN ELLISON®

An Edgeworks Abbey Offering

in association with

KICKS BOOKS
NEW YORK, NEW YORK

GETTING IN THE WIND
A very young HARLAN ELLISON®
[Author of SEX GANG (Part Two) writing as:
"Paul Merchant" and other *noms de plume*]

GETTING IN THE WIND is an original Edgeworks Abbey® offering
in association with Kicks Books.
Published by arrangement with the Author
and The Kilimanjaro Corporation.

GETTING IN THE WIND
by HARLAN ELLISON®

Harlan Ellison websites:
www.harlanellison.com and www.HarlanBooks.com

For more signed and personalized Harlan Ellison books:
c/o HERC: Post Office Box 55548, Sherman Oaks, California 91413

Published in 2012 by Kicks Books
PO Box 646 Cooper Station
New York NY 10276
Printed in the United States of America

ISBN: 978-0-9659777-7-7

Editor: Miriam Linna
Transcription and editorial asst.: Gigi Himmel
Design: Pat Broderick/Rotodesign
Front cover painting: Les Toil

www.kicksbooks.com

This one, at last,
for the rightist of
my closest, dearest
friends:

the incomparably loyal

OTTO PENZLER

maven of the world of mystery

GARDYLOO!

Traditionally, usually, conventionally, this position in the front matter of a book is site for a list of the author's *other* books, major titles, films, et al. To find such a chronology, from #1 through about #90, for Ellison... please hie thee to Pages 164-169. There is only a finite amount of space in the known universe. You may consider pp. 164-169 the variorum listing, and ever so accurate.

contents

A WORD FROM THE PUBLISHER

by Miriam Linna

BEWARE of the "pal" who offers you that first "goof ball" or "reefer" or Harlan Ellison story— "for free." Next time it won't be "for free"...

You'll be hooked—damned to a lifetime spent quieting an ever-growing craving, a twisted, clawing, tilted, gnawing desire for more... more... more *Harlan Ellison!*

Welcome to my nightmare, a twilight world where nothing seems quite right without a regular dose of attitude and anxiety from the inexhaustible tale spinner. Ellison's gift to us mortals is a murky pond populated by oddly arrogant stories drawn from the crevices of his psyche, from that sightless nut from behind where dreams spring—little journeys into lives imaginary and real, where children kill, and women maim, and good men fall prey to schemes and dreams blown 'round by a cold wind that threatens, downs, and destroys.

In PULLING A TRAIN, our first collection of rare and lost Ellisonia, we delivered the pseudonymous 1959 novella SEX GANG, and a sack of assorted deadbeat whimsy, dragged from dregs and the dung, from night-bright city swamps and fouled backstreets and office cellblocks where nylons and high heels scream and scratch, and surly is a common adjective, most certainly implied when not employed.

Now, Ellison strikes again with GETTING IN THE WIND—a mad set of decades-old stories that have avoided times and trends, and are as eternally, shamelessly human today as they were fifty years ago when they appeared in the oily pages of magazines for men—hot blooded, hen-pecked, morally vapid and physically deprived... *possibly*—but men all the same, men in need of stimulating reading material to while away the minutes and hours of emptiness that punctuate a lifetime.

Noir? Never. Fashionably perverse? Not on your life. Harlan Ellison repels the stigma of common popularity like a roach bomb in an infested food storage locker where the refrigeration unit has gone dead from a brown-out at the power grid caused by a massive solar flare and some odd alignment from *Al Kiblah*.

This stuff is deadly. It has stalked and waited in the shadows for decades—a lifetime—for a convenient moment to strike fear and dread into a placated populace. That time is now. Prepare for yesterday's tomorrow... today.

—Miriam Linna, editor
Bad Seed Magazine/Kicks Books
Brooklyn NY

INTRODUCTION

HARLAN ELLISON®

DOING IT FOR A BUCK

Many, many eons ago, before the Earth had cooled and bunny rabbits spoke vulgate Phoenician, I did a book of stories for a man I disliked. More than just "disliked" him. Came to despise him. The closer one stalks toward the pit of asps, the louder becomes the hissing. I did it for the money. For the buck. Not a lot of money, but I *did* do it to get paid. To eat. Like everyone else in the world...from your neighbor, the butcher down the block, to Leonardo da Vinci, I worked for The Man. Whoever that Man might have been. Just like you and your Mama and your Poppa. No one who works for an honest wage is a whore. Pack-mule, maybe. But not a whore.

I didn't dislike him at first, because though I had known him for some years (he had bought my very first professional submission—a cartoon I'd conceived while in East High School in Cleveland—brilliantly drawn by my pal Ray Gibson), had sold stories to him, had conned his business partners into being my pigeons at Killer Gin Rummy (taught to me by the greatest Gin grifter in the game, my late Mother, Serita R.), I didn't dislike him at first. Why *shouldn't* I like a man who had hired me straight out of the Army, who was paying me a grand a month—a lot of money in 1957—a lot of money *today*—who was buying my stories and letting me do what I loved: to edit a slick national magazine? Why did I come, within a year, of disliking him so much, I came to *despise* him?

Let me ask you The Question.

There are no wrong answers. I'll ask, you'll think about it, and you'll know which you are: The dog catcher, or the dog. I can wait all day for your answer: Here's The Question.

Have you ever worked for someone who had the whip, so they cracked it, necessarily or not? Have you ever worked for someone who *knew* you knew how to do your job, you'd been doing it for years, but kept giving you "brilliant" new ways of doing that job, even though ideas such as those had been tried decades previously and weren't as good as what was *currently* in place? Did you ever work for someone who had gotten the job who-the-hell-knows-what-exec-he-was-related-to, and should have been out raising mushrooms, keeping outta yer face and letting you get on with it? Have you ever worked for someone who knew you were having hard times—family health emergencies, bills you couldn't pay, car trouble, he *knew* you were in need of some small assistance, and sat on it, and said nothing, didn't offer, let you twist in the wind? To what good end? Didn't do him any harm to be kind, but he had the whip, and he cracked it, just because he could? Have you ever worked for someone who prowled the office or the production-floor, carrying one of those god-damned "instruments of authority," say, a clipboard, with pen at ready? Didn't do much, but he prowled, watching, efficiency expert incognito; didn't do a damned thing; but he played the narc, just to keep everybody "on their toes." Ever work for him?

Ever work for a guy who seemed to get a sexual charge out of lording it over you, keeping you on edge, watching and saying nothing? Getting his high, a secret buzz from being King Freak of control? Kind of guy who knew it all, and couldn't wait a second to jump on your ass if you made the tiniest slip? Why don't you fill in the rest of The Question here yourself?

Then, to the truth of your burning in Hell forever, which have *you* been? The dog catcher with the whip...or the cringing, whipped dog?

There was a moment when I needed about fifteen hundred bucks. After a year. I was doing great at the job, but I ran into a stumble, and I needed fifteen hundred. He spent more than that playing lousy poker. And he knew I needed it; and I was a valued producer for him. So I asked him for an advance on my salary, said I'd repay it posthaste.

He wouldn't say no.

But he wouldn't say yes.

As my situation worsened, and he watched me like a vanga-shrike beadily eyeing a small mouse it was about to impale on a blackthorn bush, he made me sweat. Made me wait. No *upside* to making me paranoid, driving me frantic, getting me angrier by the day. But he persisted, couldn't help himself, says I today, graciously. Till the afternoon he took me to lunch and told me I couldn't draw the advance...unless I did *this thing* for him. A thing he knew I didn't want to do; a thing that wasn't illegal, just so smarmy he knew it made me wanna fwow up me cookies.

But I was in dire straights.

And I did the job. No pack-mule. I whored myself.

One of my favorite quotations is from the great novelist Gustave Flaubert, who said, "Modesty is a kind of groveling." And while there is no immodesty in this introduction to youthful excesses and inadequacies, even the greatest artist was once a beginner. And as long as one works with what Guy de Maupassant called "clean hands and composure," one need never apologize. As here, one may explain the times and the context: but no need to apologize. Explanation, not craven apologia.

I have a suspicion that one of the masters who worked on the Great Pyramid of Cheops was originally only a pitiful hod-carrier, a pack-mule, who discovered that—after years of just doing the scutwork that would put matzoh on the table—he had a flair for this huge beast he was working on—managed to keep at it until he became, himself, a master, a Great Beast with the Right Stuff.

I hope to go out as a Great Beast, not merely as a hod-carrier.

But that's how I started, and this book memorializes my early struggle. An autodidact, booted out of college after only a year and a half, who read a lot, got good advice from much better writers than I, and who worked at his craft day after day, story after story, year after year.

It only comes to you *now* because Miriam Linna has been a long-time fan of the Ellison oeuvre. Great thanks go out.

If you were writing as a freelancer in the '50s (and into the 1960s, not to mention to this day) you wrote for a penny a word. Three thousand word short story, thirty bucks, one long night hitting the keys: bought you groceries for a week. It was the going rate. Some schlock publishers paid only a half-cent per word, and many higher-toned magazines like *The Saturday Evening Post* and *The New Yorker* and *Playboy* paid up to 10 cents a word; but you had to have an Olympian rep to get *that* kind of payday. I was a relative tyro at the time. An unknown packmule hod-carrier. I wrote most of the stories in this book at the start of my almost sixty-year career, for a penny a word. "Back-of-the-book" no-name. I wrote to live. Literally.

So, a few years later, I was being mustered out of the Army, having been drafted, still writing, and having crankily yet honorably served my sentence, and was about to go back to the World. I had sold a few stories while in the US Army Armor Center at Fort Knox, Kentucky, to this perfectly urbane, genteel publisher of paperback science-fantasy magazines, who was branching out into men's magazines...and he offered me the opportunity, rather than go back to the hardscrabble editorial venues of New York (whilst schlepping a rotten marriage that was falling apart around me) to come to Chicago environs, for a grand a month, to edit for him...this magazine that would (soon, I was assured) rival *Playboy*.

I took the job.

And in a few months I came to dislike him. That was a long time ago. You try hard: you try to give'm the broadest acceptance. Long time ago. 1949 to something like 1953. Worked for him twice, with a year's break, fleeing him, in there somewhere.

It's more than fifty years later as I write this, and Iditarod sled dogs unfed since the Pleistocene could not drag his name out of me, even though he's long been out of the Federal pen. (I once came close to cudgeling his apple-don't-fall-far-from-the-tree father into guava paste with a #19 Brunswick pool cue when the old man kept using the word "kike" in an anecdote as we were shooting a little one-pocket at his son's mansion. But that's another...)

I came to Chi, I got divorced, I created the books, I ran back to New York, I got married again, I got snookered into going *back* to Evanston, outside Chicago, worked on the Regency Books quality line I'd created (with which this guy had lured me back, in exchange for me pack-muling every month's mud-load of Nightstand titles) and in the process...

SEX GANG came out. I shuddered. "Paul Merchant" was a walking dead secret, a zombie buried, and never to be dug up. It was composed of stories I'd written when I was learning my craft in the early '50s. I did them as well as I could—at the time. I got a lot better as time moved along swiftly. But when I'd been writing those stories for pocket-sized digest hardboiled mystery and juvenile delinquent magazines, also *Playboy*-style men's magazines, they were crude by my later standards.

I did the book under a penname. I was ashamed to have such early work associated with the Great Rep I later established. I wouldn't make reference to it in the extensive lists of my published works, I would not sign copies at conventions if someone had pierced the veil. It was an outcast for more than fifty years.

Came to be a rare, extremely valuable ebay item, sold for lots of money to aficionados and obessives. I kept my mouth shut. By that time I was a Big Name Writer.

It's never the crime that gets you: it's the cover up.

But my cool friend in Red Hook, Miriam Linna, kept at it, wanting me to re-release the book. She likes things grotty.

So it was supposed to be one book of truly awful stories written by an autodidact who'd been thrown out of college after a year and a half, who taught himself to write on an Olympia manual typewriter with two fingers—120 words a minute, no errors.

Never to be reprinted.

I think I got a thousand bucks for it. Yeah: a grand of that desperately-needed fifteen I'd gone through hell to prise out of him after he made me twist twist twist.

It kept me eating.

But never to be reprinted. Lost. Gone. Forgotten and good riddance.

None of the above took into consideration the indefatigable Miriam Linna. And late last year she overcame my protestations, and it was supposed to be only one book of, as I said, awful stories I wrote when I was first grinding in my heels, starting out, hungry like the wolf, and needing groceries more than eminence.

Arrogant little cocksucker: I knew I had the stuff, but it had to be pulled out line by line, story by story, writing usually for a penny a word, a 3000 word story in a night while I held down two jobs in New York. But I knew I could get there, if I broke my ass.

Since then, and for more than fifty years, I labored at this machine and I learned to write good enough to wind up in the ENCYCLOPAE-DIA BRITANNICA—right between "Ellis Island" and "Ralph Ellison"—but there was that lost, forgotten blot... SEX GANG by "Paul Merchant."

Not taking into consideration Miriam Linna and Kicks Books.

So I went my way, bent over like a beanfield hand, learned to write—they tell me—better than pretty good, made that hungered-for Big Name for myself (despite my crippling humility), and now here comes Linna, back again like the Seven-Year Locust, who wants to reprint SEX GANG, wants to excavate and dig up that moldering corpse and do a Night of the Living Dead with it, for Kicks; and because she cannot be stopped. The curse of Friendshipstein.

A crappy old paperback filled with hard-nosed j.d. and men's magazine stories, with a few better ones from a later period, to plump it up: stories I wrote for that damnable penny a word. And she does it. She gussies it up so it looks good. We give it a new title that is so po-litically incorrect it made my wife threaten to leave me and, next time I blink, it has sold so well, Miriam wants to do a Book 2. Which I want to do about as much as I want an extra set of el-bows. But Miriam has decided. So: "Gee, here's a great idea: I'll do a Book 2!"

If you liked that one, you'll probably hate this one just as much. Your fault: no one held a

Glock to your head.

And Miriam needs a title for the second book, the title of the first having been in such bad taste that she'd be ranked if I didn't fulfill her dreams for Book Two. So, here's how it goes:

You been in the joint maybe a week; it's stacked four cons to a cell, twice as many as the facility was built to accommodate. One fart stretches a whole cell block.

And you're out in the yard, just shufflin', and you see a couple of dudes standing up close to the fence, talkin'. And you are such an asshole that you mosey on by, close enough to hear what they're laying down, and one of them gives you a look that stiffens your shoelaces like *al dente* spaghetti, and he says something Old School like, "Put an egg in yer shoe, an' beat it!"

But the other one says, "Get in the wind, dickwad."

Now that (without the dickwad amenity) is the title of this second foray into Wee Young Ellisonland. What it means is: "Get the fuck outta here!"

When you're not wanted, you say, "I'm gettin' in the wind."

Miriam pleaded with me to explain that to you.

Nice kid, but sometimes I want to spoon out her eyeball.

So just buy the book. Both of them. She needs the money. She's too old now to hook.

HARLAN ELLISON
a/k/a "Paul Merchant"
25 December 2011

XVIII

This Is Jackie Spinning

HI, Y'ALL, This is Jackie spinning. That's right, it's 7:00, Eastern Standard Time, and this is Jackie Whalen spinning the hot ones, the cool ones, the bop and the rock ones, and all for you, just you, little old you. And tonight's show is a real joy-popper! Be sure to stick right by that radio, kids, because as our special guest tonight Jackie has got the lovely, luscious Kristene Long, singing star of Sapphire Records, as his guest. We'll be playing Kris's new smash "Mocking Love" as well as her hit parade topper, "Shagtown Is My Town," a little later; and we'll be talking to that living doll Miss Long, as well. But right now—right now—lets hear a little of Ricky Nelson's new one.

(Fade music up)

(Jackie Whalen, a short man with a great deal of curly hair tumbling onto his forehead, almost to the eyebrow line, cues the next record and stands up behind the consoles. He stretches out of his severely Ivy League sports jacket and hangs it on the back of his chair. He unbuttons the cuffs of his piqué buttondown shirt and, scratching a wrist, rolls the sleeves up to the biceps. He pulls down the small four-in-hand knot of his conservative challis tie and unbuttons the collar of the shirt. Then, pouring a glass of water from the carafe at his left, he takes two small pink pills from the neat pile on the edge of the right-hand turntable, and tosses them off, with the water in close pursuit. His dark, angry eyes track across the control room and light on the sheer nylon-encased legs of the tall blonde sitting expectantly in the metal chair near the control booth's big picture window. He smiles at her legs, and the smile travels up carefully, slowly, till it reaches her blue eyes, where the smile has magically been transformed into a leer. She smiles back insinuatingly. "Later, baby," he tells her, licking his lips. She moves languidly in the chair, revealing a knee. Jackie Whalen reluctantly looks away from her, to the record that is almost ending. He sits down and flips a toggle switch.)

(Music up and out)

Well, that was Ricky's new one, and there's no doubt about it being number seventeen on your Top Sixty list this week. And speaking of the Top Sixty, all you tough teens, when you want a record to wile away those hours, make sure you do it at The Spindle, 6720 Seventeenth Street. All the boys out there, especially Bernie Glass the manager, they'll take good care of you. Just tell 'em Jackie sent you, and you can expect that *big* Jackie Whalen discount.

But right now here's one that your "disc Jackie" thinks will be in number-one spot real soon. In fact, if I can make a prediction, this *will* be number one. It's that new star, the voice of Rod Conlan, singing and swinging his smash hit… "I Shouldn't Have Loved You So Much!"

(Fade music up)

(He cues the next record and turns to stare at

the girl again. She grins at him and says, "Have you told your wife about us yet?" His face darkens momentarily as honest emotion shows through; then the façade of sleek, well-fed humor moves back into place and he replies, "Don't worry about it, baby. When the time comes, she'll find out." The girl stands up, smoothing the tweed skirt over her thighs, and walks to him at the console. "Gimme a cigarette," she says. As he shakes a filter-tip cigarette free of its pack, she adds, "Florey made some pretty broad hints in his column this morning. Won't she read it and wonder where you were last night?" He lights the cigarette for her with a slim sterling-silver lighter, and the affected, boyish grin spreads up his face once more. "She's not too bright, Kris. You forget I married her when I was with that dinky two hundred and fifty watter upstate. She's a farm girl…she may have read it, but it won't dawn on her that Florey meant me. She thinks I was at a retail record distributor's convention last night. Don't let it bug you; when I want her to know, she'll know. Right now I've got bigger things to worry about." The girl re-crosses to her chair and sits down. "You mean things like Camel Ehrhardt and the Syndicate?" His face once more loses its sheen of camou-flage and naked fear shines wetly out of his eyes. "You've been pushing that Conlan dog for over a week now. They're not going to like it, Jack-ie. They covered Patti Page's version with their own boy, and every other jockey's fallen in line to give *it* the big play. You're cutting your throat by pushing Conlan." Jackie Whalen pulls at his petulant lower lip and replies, "To hell with those hoods. I've got dough in Conlan, and this could be the big one for him. They won't press their luck. They're afraid I'll go to the Rackets Committee if they push me too hard. Besides, I'm working an angle. Then Conlan gets the big shove from *this* jock!" The girl grins wisely and adds, softly, "Jackie, baby, I'd hate to have to lose you so soon. Those guys don't play games. You know what they did to Fred Brennaman when he refused their stuff for his jukeboxes." Visions of a man being fished from the river, hair matted with scum and plant life, flesh white, eyes huge and watery, skitter across Jackie Whalen's mind. He sits in the comfortable foam-bottom chair, and his thoughts consume him to such a depth that only the shushing of the needle repeating in the final groove of the spinning record brings him to attention.)

(*Music down and out*)

And that was the big one for Rod Conlan, kids. "I Shouldn't Have Loved You So Much," and it's going right to the top. I've heard 'em all for a good many years, but Rod has got it locked this time, if I'm any judge.

So I hope you'll all drop over to The Spindle, 6720 Seventeenth Street, and pick up a copy of Rod Conlan's big new one, "I Shouldn't Have Loved You So Much."

And it's time now to run down the top five of the Top Sixty, kids, so here they are:

In first place is Kris Long's "Shagtown Is My Town"—and don't forget, in just a few minutes we'll be talking it up with Kristene Long herself. In second place Fats Domino's "When The Saints Go Marching In" is still holding its own, and third place this week is occupied by Sam Cooke and "Nobody Could Hate The Cha-Cha-Cha." Fourth spot goes to Steve Don and the DonBeats with "Foolin' Around Too Long" and that big fifth place goes to Rod Conlan's "I Shouldn't Have Loved You So Much." So let's catch Rod again with that smash, because we think it's bound for the million mark.

(*Music up*)

("You're really digging your grave, Jackie," the girl says, worry lines marring the ivory perfection of her forehead. "Oh, don't get on my back, Kris," he says, cueing the next record. "Sybil does the same damned thing, and I can't stand *her*." The girl winces at the comparison between herself and Whalen's wife, and settles back with the stub of her cigarette. Whalen leans over in the console chair and pulls at his lower lip, mumbling to himself. "What?" the girl asks him. "I forgot to bring that damned revolver with me today," he says. "I left it in the nightstand." The girl rises once more, walks to the console and snubs the cigarette in the large ceramic ashtray. "You might need it today," she says. It is obvious she thinks no harm can come to Whalen; it is obvious in her carriage, in her looks, in her voice. "What the hell," he says, "I'll pick it up when I go back to the apartment to change. It's safe where it is." "But are *you*?" the blonde demands. He ignores her, and watches the black disc spinning under the rapier-tip of the diamond needle. As it reaches the final grooves, he flips a switch.)

(*Music under, Announcer voice superimpose*)

…your cool lips have told me…

…I shouldn't have loved you…so-o-o mu-ch.

And that was Rod Conlan again, kids, swinging his big new one, "I Shouldn't Have Loved You So Much." After this word about Blim, the miracle cream that will rid *you* of unsightly pimples and blackheads in just one week, we'll be back to have that talk with the lovely Kris Long.

(*E.T. Commercial up*)

(He riffles through a sheaf of after-commercial comments written by the continuity department and tosses over the console, "This Blim crap couldn't remove dirt from a sand pile," to the girl. She laughs lightly, and examines a fingernail with its polish chipped. She bites at the nail absently.)

(*Commercial out, segué to Announcer*)

That's the straight stuff, kids. Blim is *guaranteed* to do the job, guaranteed to leave your skin fresh and clear and clean, or your money will be refunded. Don't miss going to that hop just because of unsightly blemishes or blackheads. Jump out right after the show tonight, kids, and fall down on a jar of that great Blim.

And now, what you've all been waiting for, let's call over that singing sensation of Sapphire Records, Miss Kristene Long, whose rendition of "Shagtown Is My Town" is holding tight to first place all around the country.

Hi, Kris.

"Hi, Jackie."

We're really thrilled to have you here today,

Kris.

"It's a big thrill to be here, Jackie."

Kris, let's get serious for a minute, and find out just how you got into the singing game. You're a lovely girl, and you look to be about—oh, about twenty-one.

"Ha-ha-ha. Why, thank you, Jackie. Actually, I'm twenty-five, and I first got my break singing with Earl Pettifore's band in Detroit. It was just a step up to singing on my own, I guess."

Well, that's really tremendous, Kris. Tell me, how do you feel about the success of "Shagtown Is My Town"?

"Jackie, I'm really thrilled. I mean it's such a great thrill to know you've recorded a song so many people like so much. When Al Hackey at Sapphire first showed it to me, I wasn't too hot about it, but Al isn't A&R man at Sapphire for nothing. He certainly—"

—Excuse me, Kris.

For all you kids out there who might not be familiar with the term, A&R means Artist and Repertory, and it's the title used by the man who selects the songs and who'll sing them. Sorry to interrupt, Kris, go on, won't you?

"—well, all I was gonna say was that Al certainly knows a hit when he hears it."

And so do we, Kris. So for all those kids out there who've made "Shagtown Is My Town" the number one song in the nation, here's Kristene Long doing her rocking, socking version of that big sensation.

(*Music up*)

(Jackie Whalen cues and then draws a cigarette from the pack and lights it. "One for me," the girl says, and he hands her the lit one from his mouth. "Much more of this kind of idiot chatter and I'll be ready for the Hysteria House," she says drawing the smoke into her lungs. He shrugs, "It's what the teenaged morons want, so who am I to argue. It's bought me a Porsche." The girl points a finger at him. "Yeah, and Florey called attention to it in that damned item. Why can't you drive a studio car when you're out with me?" Whalen rubs his lower lip with a manicured fingernail and waves her objection away. "Forget it. There's no surprises left in this life for old Jackie Whalen, baby.")

(*Music down and out*)

Kris, now that we've heard your number-one hit parade entry, what's new for you these days?

"Well, Jackie, right now I'm in town for the opening of my new movie *Holiday Rock* which opens at the Rialto tomorrow. It's my first big singing role, and working with such great stars as Fats Domino, Tommy Edwards, Joni James, Gene Vincent and The Redcaps and Bill Haley was a tremendous thrill."

Say, that is news, Kris. I know we'll all be down there for that smash premiere tomorrow at the Rialto. How about giving us that title again, Kris.

"*Holiday Rock*, Jackie."

Well, Kris, it's about time for some music, so why don't we spin that new one of yours, "Mocking Love," that has everybody so excited.

"That'd be swell, Jackie, and thanks a million."

(*Fade music up*)

(Jackie Whalen cues the next record and turns to say something to the girl, who still sits behind the spare microphone at the right-hand turntable. He stops in mid-turn, for three men are looking into the control room through the huge picture window. He sighs tightly, recognizing one of them. The girl catches the direction of his stare, and turns to look. "What's the matter?" she demands, looking between them. "Ehrhardt," he says simply, staring at the squat man in the camel's hair coat. The man has a brown snap-brim down over his eyes, and a pipe clutched tightly in a corner of his thin-lipped mouth. "I'm getting out of here," the girl cries, starting to rise. He quiets her with a vicious "Sit where the hell you are. I'll handle this. I've been—been waiting for them." He beckons to the men to enter the control room. The red **ON THE AIR** light has gone off. One of the taller, silent-faced men with Camel Ehrhardt opens the door to the control booth, and the squat man enters. "How'd you get in, Camel?" Whalen demands in a cheery, false good-humor voice. The squat man draws a metal chair up to the console and sits down. He speaks with difficulty around the pipestem. "We have ways," he says, in a cultured, dulcet tone. "We asked you to cooperate with us, Jackie. You know we have a lot of time and money behind Wally George. We hate to see all that dough going down the drain so you can make a buck off that dog Conlan." Whalen begins to speak, but the record ends. He motions to everyone for silence, noting the half-crazed expression of terror in Kristene Long's blue eyes. He flips a switch.)

(*Music out*)

That was Kris Long's big new one, "Mocking Love," kids. And here's Mitch Miller and his orchestra on the Columbia label with "The Munich Drinking Song." So, sing along with Mitch!

(*Music up, automatic gain reduces volume set too high*)

(Camel Ehrhardt draws a large, meaty hand from a patch pocket of the camel's hair coat. A .32 Police Special is clutched in the hand. "Jackie, you're going to make radio history tonight. Your listeners are going to be the first to hear a man actually die on the air." Whalen cues in the next song and settles back in the chair, and the two side men of Ehrhardt move around the console toward him. "You can't commit murder while we're broadcasting, Ehrhardt." He laughs at them. "Too many people saw you come in and too many people would see you—" Ehrhardt interrupts rudely, "*No* one saw us come in, no one sees us go out." He takes the pipe from his mouth. Jackie Whalen's full lower lip trembles and the girl is trying to suck up all the air in the booth through a big wet hole in her face. Whalen puts a flat palm against the air to ward off Camel Ehrhardt's action. "Hold it a minute, Camel. I've been waiting for you to come around to see me. Look, there's no reason why we have to be on opposite sides of this thing." The squat man cocks a heavy eye-brow. "No? Why not? Am I supposed to *like* penny-ante chiselers who take nicks out of my till?" Whalen leans forward and the bully-boys twitch with readiness to pounce on him. "Listen, Camel, you can make twice as much as you're making now." Camel Ehrhardt's face tilts querulously, and he says, "I'm listening to you." The record rasps as it catches in the last groove, and Jackie motions Ehrhardt to silence for a moment.)

(*Music down and out*)

Mitch Miller and "The Munich Drinking Song." Looks like another hit to follow "Bridge On The River Kwai March" and "Children's Marching Song." That one is really big this week. As my buddy Ed Sullivan says, "A reeeleee big shewww." Old Jackie wants to take sixty seconds now to give you the word about Sparkle Toothpaste, kids, so bend your ears around this word from Wayne Marks.

(*Commercial record up*)

("Go on," Ehrhardt says. Jackie looks at the huge clock on the wall, timing the commercial, and launches quickly into "I've got Rod Conlan and you've got Wally George. So okay, why couldn't the Syndicate—" Ehrhardt snaps, "Don't call us that!" and Whalen pales, then continues, "—why couldn't your group have *both* of them? That way you have two moneymakers going for you. And I could make you a mint on both of them, by plugging their hits." Ehrhardt's gun hand wavers, and he stares thoughfully at Whalen for a long time. "You want to cut us in on Conlan?" Jackie nods. "What percent?" Ehrhardt asks. Jackie motions him to silence, and cuts in over the commercial's fading sound.)

(*Commercial out, segué to Announcer*)

For teeth that shine like true love, kids, don't get steered onto any brand but Sparkle. It contains the miracle ingredient PAX-60 and it tastes like fresh, clean mint. So when your toothbrush is empty, don't be startled...be Sparkled!

Now here's one you've been asking for, and we're sending this one out to Angie and Phil, Marcia and Carl, Dave and Someone Special, and all the kids out at the Triangle Dairy Hop. Here it is, that new one for Jerry Lee Lewis... "Rip Tide"!

(Music up)

("Goddamnit, Whalen, what percent?" Ehrhardt asks again. The gun hand steadied. "No percent," Jackie Whalen answers, cueing and grinning hugely at the same time. The girl draws a sharp breath, and the two bully-boys cast appreciative glances at her sweater front. "Straight out sale, Camel," Whalen says. "Fifty thousand and he's yours, contract and all, with my personal guarantee that I plug the hell out of his records. As well as Wally George's stuff." The squat man licks his thin lips for a moment, and his face is a mask of imperturbability. "Why the fast change of heart, Jackie?" Ehrhardt asks. Whalen spreads his hands. "You boys don't think I'm going to buck you, *your* organization, do you? I bought Conlan's contract so I could sell it to you. I've been waiting for you to come along for a talk. I'm only sorry you waited this long and thought I was crossing you. But now that you can see I've got a good property in Conlan, I know you're businessmen enough not to knock off the goose that can lay the golden eggs for you." Ehrhardt stares solidly at Jackie Whalen. Abruptly, he slips the still-silent weapon back into his coat pocket. With marked slowness he lights his pipe with a kitchen match. He shoves the chair back and stands up. "I'll be talking to you." He nods sharply to the sideboys and the three men leave the control booth. As Jackie Whalen reaches for the pickup arm of the turntable the three men pause outside the window, and stare at him.)

(Music down and out)

That was "Rip Tide" and it was Jerry Lee Lewis smashing. Don't forget, The Spindle, 6720 Seventeenth Street, where you can buy all these hits with that big Jackie Whalen discount. Hits like this one: Frankie Avalon and "Sweetlips."

(Music up)

(Jackie Whalen sits in silence, lips pressed tightly closed, eyes also tightly closed, the lips trembling slightly. The girl makes a sound, a half-formed word, but he waves her to silence, then rubs his eyes with his finger tips, fiercely. He waits in darkness for the record to end. When it does he cuts in abruptly.

(Music down and out; cut to Announcer)

Well, today has been a big day, kids. Bigger than you know, really. And I see by the big clock on the wall that it's almost 8:00, time for your disc Jackie to close down the old shop and say so long till tomorrow. We've just got time for two more, so I'll lay 'em on together and let 'em run out to close the show. We don't usually

hit a platter as hard as we're hitting these two,
kids, but today has been a real special day, so
we'll break our own rule. Here they are, because
you've made them your favorites.

Here's Rod Conlan again with that hit you've
been phone-bombing us to play more often, "I
Shouldn't Have Loved You So Much" and the
extra-beautiful Kris Long with "Mocking Love,"
what I predict will be the two big ones of the
season.

(Music up)

(Jackie Whalen stands, scratches at himself,
and walks to the chair in which Kristene Long
sits, her back very straight, her face very pale.
"You lead a real rough life, Mr. Whalen," she
says. He leans down, takes her face in his hands
and kisses her full on the lips. "You'll find out
just *how* rough tonight, baby." He grins. Jackie
Whalen straightens, reaches back and takes the
pack of cigarettes from the console. He shakes
one out. With the smoke full in his lungs he replies to her unasked questions: "It was a calculated risk, honey. I knew they'd come around to
dicker first. The days of the St. Valentine's Mas-
sacre may not be gone completely, but these
guys are businessmen, even though they're
hoods and punks. They won't pass up a chance
to get hold of good property like Conlan. They'll
come across; I made a sale today. That was the
angle I was playing." The girl shakes her head.
"They'll sell him down the river. Lousy songs
with big pushes, too many personal appearances, too many bookings for benefits, they'll

screw him good, Jackie. They always do." Whalen shrugs and sits on the edge of the console. "That's the way it goes," he says. "It was either him or me. And he'll like working for the Syn— for the group.")

(*Segué first record into second*)

(The girl stands up and half turns away, tucking a lock of blonde hair that has tumbled over her forehead back into place. As she turns she faces the big control booth window and sees a short, dark woman in a beret and black coat, standing in the center of the glass, staring at them. A peculiar expression trembles on the woman's face. She is holding a gun out before her, stiffly. "Jackie!" the girl shrieks. Whalen turns and sees the woman. "Sybil!" he gasps, as she brings the gun up an inch. Thoughts pile through Jackie Whalen's head as the gun travels that inch. They are jumbled, disorganized thoughts. One is:

She *did* understand who Florey was talking about in his column. Another is:

How did she find the revolver in the night stand? A third is:

How stupid: to make it past one bunch of killers who make their living knocking guys off, just to get it from a stupid, jerky farm girl. Oh, Jeezus! And the last thought of all is:

There are no more surprises in this life for Jackie Whalen.

And as the crash of the revolver echoes through the anteroom, into the control booth, as the glass of the picture window magically sprouts three small bullseyes with millions of radiating lines, as fire and pain and chagrin and cursing fill Jackie Whalen like an empty vessel...)

(Music fade up and GONE. EXTREMELY GONE.)

Dead Wives Don't Cheat

(as by "John Magnus")

HE WAS DAMNED tired of her lousy bickering, her threats of infidelity, so he shut her up for good. He strangled her noisily in bed—while her unbelieving eyes took one last baby-blue look at him.

He didn't want to look at her after he'd done it. Instead, Weiman poured a shot of scotch and dashed it against the back of his throat. It had never tasted so good. He put on his pants and found a clean shirt in the dresser. The over-starched collar scratched against his perspiring neck, made him feel like tearing it off, stuffing it down her sweet, choked, lily-white throat. But he didn't want to look at her again. He figured he earned the right not to.

The sun was just coming up when he smoothed the last lock of hair into place, and squinted his eyes, taking a final look in the mirror. *I don't look like a murderer, that's for sure,* he thought.

He looked more like a wealthy importer. A little scrawny, perhaps, but definitely with the air of a man who was used to money. And at last he was going to have a chance to use it.

He flicked out the light in the bathroom, took his hat from the rack on the closet door, and crossed the bedroom. The rising sun managed to squeeze a few beams through the venetian blind, throwing a bright pattern of light across the heap in the bed. He couldn't keep his eyes off it any longer.

She had been a beautiful little bitch. She'd been on magazine covers till last year. The light showed her bare, high breasts, that had so often been concealed by little more than a puff from an air-brush, in the many "art" magazines she'd modeled for. The long, blond hair fell over her face, concealing the astonished pain which had been frozen on her face. He didn't like the idea of vultures finding her like that, naked in bed, but he didn't have time to dress her now.

He pulled the blanket out from under her feet, and covered the contorted body up to the neck. He turned away quickly.

The corner of his mouth slid upward with a little quiver, and dispersed the grimly determined mood which had shadowed his face. He almost laughed. When he had been younger, it had been called a sensitive face. The pampered face of a rich kid used to the luxuries his father's import trade could provide. There wasn't as much money as in the old days, Weiman thought, but he had still outdone the old man in his own way. He wouldn't have to wait until *his* own cheap, blathering whore of a wife—somewhere down the pike, probably— made him old before he could have a real thing. His father had sat in decay and waited, his hate making him a feared man in business. Ernest Weiman Jr. had sat in silence and planned.

He closed the door carefully.

Weiman opened the door of the private

elevator, and felt the good, normal sinking in his stomach as he left the penthouse behind forever. No more of her threatening to cheat when he went on one of his overseas trips. She was the one who was taking the trip this time— and he had no doubt where to.

He remembered the sound of her mother's voice when he'd come back the last time. The elevator had brought him up, but he'd waited without opening the door when he heard voices. The silent private elevator, the penthouse, had all paid for themselves in those few seconds.

"Just one more year," he had heard her mother screeching like an unoiled hinge, "and you can dump the fool for fifteen-hundred dollars a week! You can get yourself a real husband, and have some children! That stuff you're using isn't foolproof, you know, and I don't want to have his miserable things for grandchildren!"

"I don't know whether I can take it another year," Diana had said. "He's the biggest slob I've ever seen. You should see the disgusting things he wants me to do! Why couldn't I have gotten a *handsome* millionaire?"

He'd heard the fat, peroxided mother tapping her pudgy foot on the floor. "The lawyer says one more year, darling," she had whined. "It's worth $75,000 a year, when you've taken as much as you have already!"

Weiman had waited for the conversation to change, then he'd picked up his trunks with a clatter and barged into the plush penthouse, grumbling some manufactured oaths about the Communist blockade or Chinese free trade.

He'd felt nauseated when he'd had to smile at the mother. If Diana looked like that in twenty years—if she just had those crumby genes somewhere under her perfect skin—

But he didn't have worry about that anymore. Or about her having been well-used before he'd married her.

Weiman abruptly broke out of his reverie as the elevator stopped and automatically opened into the lobby.

He paced out briskly in his good *morn*ing pace and gestured to the bellhop.

He peeled a ten-dollar bill from the folded sheaf in his pocket and tucked it into the bellboy's pocket.

"Charley, old man," he said cheerily, "bring my car around front, won't you? Don't worry about gas. I'm just going down to the dock. Leaving for Panama for a week or so. Have a big outlet down there, you know, and this border trouble is cutting off supplies. Take a cab down and bring the car back at twelve. There'll be another ten in the glove compartment for you."

The bellhop snapped a *Yes Sir, Mr. Weiman,* and trotted out the rear service entrance of the hotel to remove the black Cadillac from the hotel lot.

Weiman chuckled to himself. *Let her cheat while I'm away this time! Just let her!* He hurried out through the glass doors of the hotel as the Cadillac pulled up.

"Thanks, Charley," he said to the bellhop. "I'll see you—soon, unless I run into some shooting down there, or get captured by the underground. That could easily happen to a man in my position, you know. They've even threatened my wife to scare me away—but she'll be all right with the private elevator and everything. Just don't let anyone else up there."

He cracked another self-satisfied smile and roared away toward the harbor. He didn't notice the bellhop's knowing grin. Weiman wasn't the only one with money who had known Diana. Locked doors don't take money, but hotel bellhops seldom refuse it. As for Diana, she was willing—as long as she was able.

The sea was beginning to make itself felt against the side of the ship when Weiman appeared on deck. He handled his load easily.

The silver path of the moon's reflection was beginning to break up on the wind-tossed waves. *It doesn't make much difference,* he thought. *I'll only be in the water for a few minutes.*

Rosario was following the ship's wake in the whirlybird now. Weiman tried to listen over the rumble of the ship's engines, but he couldn't hear anything.

He crept along the starboard rail, now pulling the large bundle behind him, and carrying a thick briefcase under his free arm. He felt his way until his hand caught the line he had kicked under the rail earlier in the day.

Weiman ran through the details once more in his mind. The next day, a man would appear with his credentials at the port of Panama. He would be arrested, then released three days later when the fingerprints came back from

Washington. By that time, he would be safe in a plush, anonymous penthouse on the French Riviera.

He had twenty good years left anyway, and nothing on which to spend the six million American dollars but women, wine and more women. *Only one person is getting cheated on this deal,* he thought, patting the stuffed waterproof briefcase. *And she's too dead to care.*

Carefully, he lifted the limp, deflated raft over the rail of the boat. He took a last quick look around, and searched the sky beyond the vessel. He broke off a small stud with his thumb. The tubes inflated immediately from the bottles of gas attached to the valves of the raft. The raft struck the water with a dull slap, and the growing waves began to slosh against the tautly-inflated rubber.

Weiman unbuckled his belt, strung it through the briefcase handles, and buckled it again. Then, one pipestem leg after the other, he climbed over the railing.

He grasped the thin rope which hung down from the railing, and let himself slowly down into the raft. He put his foot flat to the hull of the ship—and pushed away hard.

Soon the ship became a shrinking black hulk behind him, and the pounding of the motors became more and more distant. Weiman took a small packet of green fluorescent powder from his vest pocket and emptied it over the edge of the boat.

He waited, staring up into the darkened sky.

At first, he didn't hear anything but a vague, soft *chunk-chunk-chunk*...distant. Then he felt a wind across his head and shoulders, a shadow passed overhead, the faint whirring sound became louder and louder; then, finally relieved, thankful, he heard the full insistent putt-putt of the helicopter overhead.

Abruptly, a floodlight was on him, bathing a circle of water in brilliance. As the 'copter came nearer, he began to make out its outlines.

A voice: "Weiman!"

It was Rosario all right. The damn gigolo even had a handsome-sounding voice. But Weiman knew he was dead-honest with him. Rosario was the only one of his "protection" men he'd trust with his life. The only thing he loved more than money was women, and Weiman made sure he had plenty of the former to supply the latter. Weiman was no fool; he knew he had to keep his men happy.

"Mr. Weiman!" shouted the voice, with a resonance that nearly made Weiman afraid it would be heard from the ship. "I'm here on time, eh? We make hurry to Habana, and take you on the big plane to France."

There was a peculiar urgency to Rosario's voice that Weiman hadn't heard before. Of course, he had never seen him in action.

The rope ladder danced just out of Weiman's reach. He stood up halfway in the raft, straining his aging muscles toward the skillfully-handled craft.

Rosario's clean-cut face appeared in the cab doorway. He began to lower the thin rope with a small hook on the end toward Weiman. "Put the briefcase on the hook, Mr. Weiman. Then you can come up the ladder."

Weiman leaned over and reached with one hand toward the rope. He undid his belt, removed the briefcase, and carefully put it on the lowered hook. Rosario began to pull it up again. "It is very heavy, Mr. Weiman. You must have a great deal of money."

Weiman stared up at the grinning face. "Yes, I have a very great deal of money, and soon much of it will be yours, Rosario!"

The Latin grinned again as he took the briefcase off the hook. Weiman could make out his features clearly in the cab's control board glow. Rosario hefted the briefcase in one hand, and it disappeared into the cabin of the helicopter.

"Goodbye, Mr. Weiman. Maybe I come back once in a while, see you drown, huh? You lousy bum, Mr. Weiman, I don't like you!" Rosario's face had suddenly become dark and angular in the reflected light from the cabin.

Weiman's face dropped. Alarm spread up his body. "Rosario! You know I always treat you good! What are you doing? Holding out for more money? I'll give you five thousand dollars more. You can own half the whores in New York. Come on, Rosario. You know I'm going to treat you right!" The harsh light played weird effects on his contorted face.

Rosario peered down from the helicopter. His face flamed with hate. "You bum!" he screamed. "You don't give me no fair deal at all! That woman you kill this morning. I have my last date with her before I go away with you, and I find her dead! Dead! Dead and naked in bed with your picture in the room. You tell me you kill your wife! You kill my woman! I take no money for that! I love her, and I'll kill you for it!"

Weiman stood up in the raft and screamed, "Rosario! My wife! Good God, you slept with my wife when I was gone! I'll kill you, Rosario! Somehow I'll kill you!" His face was red, flaming with impotent rage. He was hunched over like an animal ready to spring.

Rosario pulled a .38 from his black leather flying jacket, fired three times, rapidly. Weiman, sallow and incredulous, sat down in the middle of the sinking raft. Air rushed out of the tube from the six jagged holes in the rubber.

Water began to trickle in through the tunnels in the collapsing rubber tube.

The helicopter suddenly revved up and huge billows washed over the tiny craft. Weiman looked up helplessly, his mouth wide open.

Rosario's head thrust through the window again. "Now you have your way, bum! Nobody ever solve the murder. Now comes my time. You leave her there to cheat three weeks out of four, then kill her. She was fine, I tell you, except the dirt you left on her!" Weiman's mouth was still open. He stared ghost-eyed. "You look like skinny, stuffed pig, Mr. Weiman," Rosario yelled above the blur of the rotors. "You mouth open where the apple should be!"

The raft suddenly gave way, and Weiman stood up on the sinking wad of rubber, looking for a moment as though he were standing knee-deep in a puddle.

With a deafening roar, the helicopter whirled high into the air...and vanished into the night.

Pride in the
Profession

THERE WERE MANY who called the lynching of Eustace Powder a blot on the previously unbesmirched reputation of Princetown, but for Matthew Carty, it was the handing-down of a latter day Ten Commandments.

The alleged crime for which the dusty Negro was swung high is of no consequence at this time; suffice it to say he was innocent, if not in thought, at least in deed, indeed; but all things pass, and the momentary upheavals that result in the neck-stretching of onc unimportant dark man are of no importance in the shadow of later, more electric events.

For it was the excitement, the crowd-respect directed at the man who knotted the rope and threw it over the elm's thick branch, that struck eight-year-old Matt Carty with such lasting force. The humid, expectant rustle of the summer day, the pavement warm beneath his bare, dirty feet, the women watching flame-eyed. It was all such a rich experience, he could not put it from him.

There was even an unexpected touch of homespun humor. The black, black man's last request, jocularly offered by one of the local rakehells, was to have a pair of dice, to hold in his hand when they swung him aloft. "Those who live by the bones gonna *die* by the bones!" replied the last-request-man, and fishing in his own jeans, he came up with a fine cubed set of red plastic dice; as neat as a set of see-through galloping dominoes as ever was. And giving them to Eustace Powder, the local happysmith patted the Negro on the cheek. "Roll a natural, boogie," he grinned, and the black man clenched them in his fist tightly as they yanked him aloft.

The face of the gap-toothed Eustace Powder, his mouthings of horror and expectation. The gurgle and retching and final gasp as he swung clear of the ground. He seemed to thrash and twitch interminably. It was one of the two high points of Matt Carty's life, even if Powder *did* drop one of them.

In light of that one incident, his existence was systematically directed, till the day he died, many years later.

For Matt Carty *liked* the idea of being a hangman.

There was a certain pride a man could take in such a profession. So he took pride, and he took the profession. It suited him, and he suited it. A wedding of the right job with the proper tool.

Matt Carty had always been a little man. Not a small man, for that is a thing of personality, and Matt's personality was just fine, thank you. He was outgoing and dryly witty, with perception to temper it; but this was too much offset by his lack of height—an almost comical lack. He was five feet one inch tall.

He had often considered elevator shoes. Only the inherent hypocrisy of them prevented their purchase. In their place he substituted an almost pathetic eagerness for love and friendship. Indiscriminately, Matt Carty made friends.

Unfortunately, they did not stick to him for long:

"Jeeze, it's real funny, meeting a guy from Princetown here in Chi. I mean, me being a guy from Henshaw, I mean that's only twenty-six miles, an' this is a helluva big town. Wanta 'nother drink, Matt?"

"Oh, golly, no. So tell me—uh, what was it? Harold?—Harold, tell me, what are you doing here in Chicago?"

"I'm a buyer for a linoleum house. You know, I price rolls and cuttings. How about you?"

"I'm at the U. of C."

"No *kidding*?"

"Uh-huh. Studying plane geometry and advanced engineering design."

"What line are you in?"

"I'm a hangman."

"—uh?"

"That's right. I'm a professional executioner. I work free-lance for the states. Of course, I haven't had too many jobs to my credit, but, well, *you* know…you've got to start somewhere. You see, I'm studying the mathematics of falling weights, and the force of vectors so when I—say, where are you going?"

"—uh—I just saw an old friend of mine, a business acquaint—I, uh, gotta go. Say, it was real swell meeting you; take it easy, huh?"

End of friendship.

With love, it was considerably more difficult. Being a normal, red-blooded American lad, Matt Carty sought the companionship of attractive young women. But in that case, also, it was star-crossed:

"Matty, pl*eeee*ase!"

"Aw, c'mon, Jeannie."

"Now, Matthew Carty, if you don't take your hand out of there, I'm getting out of this car this *minute*!"

"I thought you loved me..."

"...welll...I *do*, but..."

"But what?"

A prolonged silence.

"Isn't the night cool, Jeannie?"

"Mmmm."

"It was on nights like this that the hangmen of Henry the First's period prepared their scaffolds."

"What a perfectly *sick* thing to think about, Matt."

"Why, what's sick about it? I think it's a real fine thing to think about. I mean, after all, it *is* my line of work."

"Your *whaaat*?"

"I, uh...heh-heh..."

"You told me you were in lumber!"

"Heh-heh..."

"What, *exact*ly, do you do for a living, Mr. Carty?"

"I'm a, uh, well, I'm a h—"

End of love.

But the hazards of the trade were offset by other, more ephemeral, pleasures. There was the pleasure of the feel of good hemp stretched taut. There was the satisfying *rightness* of a great weight swinging free, like a pendulum, at the end of a straight plumb. There was the heady

wine of sound produced by the progression of
an execution:

Feet mounting scaffold.

Milling about.

Monotoned prayers.

Man puffing cigarette.

Adjustment sounds, most precise.

Trap release.

The door banging free.

The *thwuumpppp!*

The *twannnng!*

The sound of silence.

From the first tentative stirrings within
him, the subliminal cravings for recognition—
recognition in the field he had chosen—
Matt Carty had gone about the business of
preparation properly. First high school, with
emphasis on woodworking (incase of do-it-
yourself emergencies), mathematics, abnormal
psychology, dynamics of geometry and a fine
grounding in biology—one must know the
merchandise with which one works.

Then college, with several architecture
courses, penology, criminology, group behavior
classes, ethics, advanced vector analysis and
even biochemistry. He did not stay long at any
one university, however, and as a consequence,
he never came up with a degree of any sort.
How could he, with the variegated courses
he undertook, a smattering of one, at spray-
exposure to another.

And oddly enough, there were no deterrents
to his career. His parents at first expressed
white-faced horror and complete refusal of

cooperation. But they were much to involved with their own problems—she with her religion composed of unequal parts of hypochondria and incipient nymphomania, and he with *his* God: the Mighty Green Buck—so they sent young Matthew to the schools he wished to attend.

Thus he observed the slaughtering of cattle, watching carefully as they were weighed and hung. He sat in at executions. His eyes were constantly on watch for stresses and effects brought about by pressure and deadweight. He carried on harmless experiments.

He went to study at Columbia, and fell in with a disparate clique of Greenwich Village bohemians, one of whom was a bottle-auburn brunette named Carinthe who inducted him into the mysteries of sex and liquor, narcotics and bad poetry, and who cast him aside, huskless, some months later, leaving him with a bruised id and a resolute determination to become the first hangman in history to bring neck-stretching out as a sincere art-form.

Soon enough, for he was—as noted— perceptive and diligent, he developed a certain efficiency and style in the matters of hangmanship. So, figuratively speaking, he hung out his shingle.

He offered himself—after his first bonding— to the state of New Hampshire. His rate was reasonable, his manner quick and orderly, and the job was dispatched with aplomb and a certain grace. His reputation was very much like a summer virus: it spread to odd places and sank deep.

———•———

By the time he was an unwrinkled thirty, Matthew Carty was known as "that hanging man" and he had acquired a scent of fame that was responsible for articles in *The Saturday Review*, and *The American Penologist*. He was known as "that hanging man."

There were high points, of course, as there must be in all careers of note:

The celebrated swinging of "Lousy" Harry Gottesman, the helicopter-employing rustler, in Montana. His was a singular case: Mr. Gottesman weighed three hundred and sixteen pounds. It brought Matthew Carty to the notice of law enforcement agencies in each of the (then, nine; now seven) states and two territories where hanging was the accepted form of capital punishment. And, until they became states, switching to life imprisonment, Hawaii and Alaska as well. Gottesman's demise was achieved with a facility and care that could only be arranged by a genius in his field.

In his way, Matthew Carty had become the Picasso of the scaffold.

There was an all-expense-paid trip to Hawaii, in the sixth year of his fame, sponsored by the local government, to perform what the officials called an "*Aloha* ceremony" on Miss Melba Rooney, a four-timer poisoner of husbands, not all of them her own.

There was the notoriety gained from the Restout Case, and its accompanying grueling activity on the part of Utah state police to locate Algernon Restout's victim, a certain Miss Mamie Helf, known locally as an exotic dancer. Mr. Restout had separated the well-known belly dancer from her equipment—with a meat cleaver.

Public sentiment was high on that occasion; the bleachers were packed, and the popcorn sales were a local record high; Matthew Carty fulfilled his obligation to an attentive audience.

In each case, and to each hanging, Carty brought a certain indefinable gentleness and *savoir-faire* that were identifiable to the perceptive as an unflagging pride of his profession.

He was the best, and there was no getting around it.

Then, when he had begun soaking his plates in warm salt water, when he had acquired a sturdy set of grouse-tracks around his eyes and nose, when he had been warned by his doctor to move slowly in protection of an aging heart, when he was, in short, in the thickening of his lifetime, he was called to create history.

It was several months after he had completed the execution of a certain gunrunner named Moxlossis, who had butchered his partner with an icepick over a center cut of *filet mignon* on the cruise back from Cuba, when the Governor of the state of Delaware contacted him.

By official conveyance, Matthew Carty was brought to the state house, and in secret session with the governor—that year a rather paunchy man with a predilection for cigarillos and fetid breath—was informed he was to preside at the hanging of Dr. Bruno Kolles.

Matthew Carty's aging heart leaped into his wrinkled throat. The culmination of a glorious career! The *pièce de résistance*!

Matthew swallowed heavily, and swung his short legs in the air with unrestrained emotion. It was a high-legged chair, and though he felt awkward, this was news enough to sublimate his feelings of awkwardness.

The Kolles case was a *cause célèbre*. The tabloids had been publishing steadily on the matter, publicizing his arrest and conviction for over seven months:

Anna Pasteur had been a cancer victim. Her days had been numbered and her body was wasting away. It had been a body loved with singular ardor by Dr. Kolles, and as a result of the strain and horror visited upon the good Doctor at sight of his paramour wasting away, a mercy killing had been performed, her hand locked in his throughout the activity with hypodermic and sleep-inducing drug.

It had been quick and with sweet terror. But he had been discovered in the act by a jealous nurse, a remarkably horsey woman he had several times rebuffed, and she had turned him in. The case had been followed with much accompanying conjecture and opinion from all sides.

It was, in fact, the situation that the country was divided in its feelings. Half the people believed he should be turned loose—for his had been an act of compassion, easily understood and condoned—and half believed he should be hanged with brutal speed.

Thus it was that the Governor of the state of Delaware (chewing on a fetid cigarillo) told Matthew Carty, "We cannot chance a slip-up in this matter. Public sentiment is too strong." There was a detectable note in the Governor's voice, vaguely reminiscent of subdued hysteria. "You can do a speedy job, without trouble, can't you?"

Matthew assured him he could. He was most convincing. The tariff on this execution was slightly higher than usual, for the prestige was greater.

Prestige, yes, but more! This was the high point of a career marked by high points.

On the morning of the execution, Matthew felt strange quivers in his stomach. He told himself it was the nervousness of his *greatest* job, his most exacting bit of artistry. It was Leonardo completing *La Gioconda*; it was Wilbur and Orville on that chilly morning near Kitty Hawk; it was Melville, cribbing out painfully the last magnificent lines of MOBY DICK.

He felt like Icarus soaring toward the sun.

The public notice—which would not be removed until after the inquest—had been posted some twenty hours before. The demonstrators had been staunchly turned back from the prison walls. The sheriff, jailor, chaplain and surgeon of the prison all were present, as well as several dry-faced relatives, resigned to the fate of Dr. Kolles.

Matthew Carty made a point of never meeting

the man (or woman) he was to execute, but today was something special, something remarkable, so he went to the cell in the late afternoon, rubbing his chin warily.

He wanted to meet the man who was soon to be the most intimately involved with his art. It seemed fitting, though oddly disquieting, somehow.

Kolles was a short, fat man. Not quite as short as Matthew, but still under five-and-a-half feet. He had a fine hairline mustache that seemed almost hesitant about its own existence, and he took the impending stretching of his neck with restrained impotence.

"Are you the man who is going to do this thing?"

Matthew nodded. "I thought I'd come in and say I'll make it as quick as I can."

Kolles bowed his head. A red flush came up from inside his shirt and clouded his face. "What kind of man *are* you?" he asked with a quiet fury. It was the first sign of emotional strain he had evinced since the beginning of his trial. "I'm a man who tried to save lives … but … *you*! You *take* them, without apparent compunction."

Carty stared at him silently for a moment. Then he leaned down and stuck his uncomplicated face into the Doctor's. "I'm a craftsman," he explained. "My idol has always been Henry I of England. Do you know why? Because he furthered the cause of hanging. He was a great man, and his life has given me inspiration. I'm an artist, Doctor. My work is important. I take a great deal of pride in it, because I'm the best in my field.

"Can you understand that?"

None of it made much sense, and of course the good Doctor did *not* understand.

Dr. Kolles turned his face to the wall.

Matthew Carty left the cell, and went out to the courtyard where the white pine scaffold rose in clean-limbed serenity. This was the first time he had been talked to like that since the days of his rude beginnings, when the girls had slapped him and turned grey at mention of his beloved trade. The days before fame had made him tolerable, if *not* socially acceptable. He had encysted himself, and this stripping off of his shell left him raw and unprotected. He shuddered to himself.

The fools, he thought, *they could never understand me.*

He checked the sash weights and the oiled trap. He checked the arm and the lever and the floorboards for squeaks—which made an unpleasant effect of jollity when he was struggling so earnestly for somberness and seriousness. Yes, everything was in readiness.

Kolles would drop eight feet before the breaking strain. And served him right.

Yet that nervousness, compounded with the annoyance generated by the Doctor, and the pressure of the event itself, further unsettled Matthew Carty. He began to perspire for the first time in his life.

He found himself biting his perfect little nails.

How glorious today would be—his ultimate triumph!

When they brought Kolles out, with the

newsmen trailing along behind (and that hideous sob-sister from the New York paper, with her frock much too gay for this occasion) something seemed to frazzle inside Matthew. For as Kolles emerged out of shadow, he stuck his tongue out at Matthew Carty.

Carty was much too surprised to be flabbergasted.

It was very much like that time in Alaska, up past White Horse, when he had had to thaw out the hemp in a bucket of boiling water before he could do the job. Or the time in Kansas when the fall had been too great and had pulled the prisoner's head off. He had been unnerved then, too, but he had been much younger and his confidence had returned, buoyed up.

But now…

Was he getting old, unsure of himself? Had he lost his confidence in his talent?

He swallowed heavily, and strung Kolles up.

Kolles stuck his tongue out once more.

"*Stop that!*" Matthew hissed under his breath, but Kolles just smiled cherubically.

The execution would be accomplished by the fracturing or dislocating of the first three cervical vertebrae, hence crushing the vital centers of the spinal cord.

Matthew heard the music of lyre, sackbut, and dulcimer.

He placed the knot behind the ear for the most symmetrical garrote. It was more artistic than the method favored by lesser talents—under the neck.

(In point of fact, Matthew favored the *thuggee*

three-knot method as used in India. He had made an extensive study of choke methods in his exuberant youth, but had, in later life, realized the truth of tried and true old-fashioned approaches.)

His joy was constrained, but enormous. His fingers sang at his work.

He did not notice the knot slip around, as he moved away.

Perhaps it was unsteadiness of hand.

Perhaps the glory of this event in his career had made him incautious, unwary.

Perhaps he was not aware of the stress on the rope.

Perhaps Kolles jiggled a bit, out of spite.

Any of these are possibilities.

In any case, when the lever was thrust home, and the trap sprang open beneath Kolles, and he plummeted the eight feet to *twaaaang* at the end of the line, he did not break his neck. He did not die. Obstinately!

The sob-sister screamed and messed her gay frock.

The newsmen's faces screwed up hideously in expressions of compounded horror, as their eyes moved click and click, back and forth, as though they were watching a tennis match in slow motion.

The jailor turned puce, then grey, and fled.

The chaplain began praying.

And Dr. Kolles twisted and writhed and bounced and danced and flopped and tumbled about at the end of the hemp. The hanging was a ghastly fiasco...obstinately endless...it went on for a lifetime and a half, in Matthew Carty's mind. The condemned man seemed determined to kill himself slowly. The corpse did not become a corpse for a very long while.

Everyone stood transfixed, not moving, almost blind with the ghastliness of it all. Execpt the jailor, who continued running till he spanged against a barred door some distance down the hall and was knocked totally unconscious.

After a while, someone croaked, "Get a kn-knife...cut him d-d-down..."

But no one did. They just stood and watched the airborne gavotte.

In actuality, it was a mere three minutes, but it was a week to each of the horrified observers.

The newspapcrs called him an "incompetent."

The Huntley-Brinkley Report referred to him as a "butcher."

One Sunday morning egghead commentator labeled him a "male Ilse Koch!"

The women's league impeached him as a "paid murderer."

In all, it was a serious blow, a killing blow to Matthew Carty's career. For Matthew Carty knew the truth; the truth that lived inside simple appearances. He was not inept. Till Dr. Kolles, he had not felt one way or the other about his "participants" in the act. They had merely been utensils, specified by the authorities as the correct instrument for the assignment. Till Dr. Kolles. He had made the mistake of meeting the man, and from Kolles's loathing of what Matthew Carty did for a living had been born the first stench-weed of hate in the little man.

Matthew Carty had allowed himself to become personally involved with Kolles. He had hated, and that had thrown him off his stride. He knew he was washed up. Hung up, really. He knew he had lost his touch. His time had come and gone. He had met each challenge with skill and pride in his profession, but all that was dust now.

He was a has-been.

Because it was a rather small room, and because he had closed and locked all the windows, and because it was a very hot August, and because he had done it to excess, and because the cleaning woman didn't come for a week, putrefaction had progressed considerably and, when she came to clean Matthew Carty's apartment, the smell was overpowering. When she called the custodian and he unlocked the door, and they entered, they began to gag and had to step back into the hall to tie handkerchiefs over their noses.

It was the cleaning woman who first entered the bedroom. When she saw him, she tried to jam her fist into her mouth to stop the screams, but the handkerchief prevented the movement and her hysterical shrieks brought the custodian.

Even the police were shocked and surprised.

He had done it to excess. The bloodstains and brownish material he had vomited were all over the bed. The mouth was corroded and scarred, as well as the throat. He had convulsed so terribly that he was arched back into a perfect bow, the entire weight of his small body resting on the heels and back of the head. His skin was very gray and in places dark blue. The final grimace was the one most commonly associated with lockjaw. The hands had ripped the sheets.

Everyone knew who he was, what he was famous for, and none of them could understand the fierce, unrelenting pride in his profession a man could possess that would cause him—as was revealed in the autopsy—to drink a bottle of household ammonia, swallow a half-box of DDT-laden plant poison, and swallow eleven grains of strychnine sulphate.

That hanging man was dead. Pride in his profession. Not even at the end had he compromised his craft; he had *poisoned* himself.

Portrait of the Artist as a Zilch Writer

(as by "Paul Merchant")

TOMMY DENNISS LOOKED AGAIN at the little slip of notepaper on which he had jotted the address. He wasn't quite sure he had transcribed it correctly from the phone conversation. When Gordon Mills, editor of *Kingpin* (The Magazine of Lively Entertainment For Lively Men), had called him to drop into the office, Tommy had choked up inside. This was the first real, honest-to-God writing break he'd had in two years of struggling. New York was a hard row to hoe, and no matter what fiction markets he tried to crack, he always got the same thing. Rejects.

Nothing but rejects.

But now it seemed an editor wanted to purchase some of his stories. *Kingpin* was a big magazine in the urban men's field; stories to them brought three, sometimes even four hundred dollars. It was the break Tommy needed. He knew he was a good, competent commercial writer, but ever since leaving the University and coming to New York, he'd batted himself against the net with total futility.

He was determined to break in this time; working full-time as a shipping clerk in Bloomingdale's, and writing at night was rugged. He wanted more than anything to see his name in type... see letters from readers about his stuff... carry an attaché case... stop working as a clerk and start to write full-time. He was determined this time, and things looked good. He had sent three stories to *Kingpin*, and though Mills had not mentioned any of them in their brief phone conversation, Tommy was sure at least one—probably more, because they were the most significant he'd written so far—fitted the magazine nicely.

At least, he was certain he'd made an impression.

Editors just didn't call writers if they weren't interested. At least, that was what he had been led to believe.

He looked again at the room number on the paper, and followed the progression of numbers down the hall and around the corner. It was there, all right. At the end of the corridor. He strode purposefully toward the two big glass doors, but as he neared them, as he drew close enough to read

KINGPIN PUBLISHING CO., INC.
Publishers of:
KINGPIN MAGAZINE
ROCK 'N' ROLL DIGEST
REVELATIONS MAGAZINE

in heavy black on the glass, his step faltered. Tommy Denniss was a big man, over six feet, with soft curly brown hair clipped short the collegiate way, and his clothes were almost *too* conservative Ivy League. Most of the latter he had brought along from the University, but after two years of not having enough money to really buy any new ones, they were getting pretty baggy. The leather patches on his elbows were not merely for ornament.

Because of a mixed number of these factors, he grew nervous, as he drew closer to the office. Finally he stopped outside, his shadow on the glass, and fingered the four-in-hand knot of his challis tie.

He summoned up energy from the same pool that had been his source for two years. With more than drive—more like an inner desire he could constantly feel pulsing within him—Tommy Denniss opened the door and walked in.

"I was wondering how long it would take you to open it," she said.

Tommy stood in the open doorway, staring at the girl behind the reception desk. It had been made for her, that desk. It was cut out for the knees, and she had crossed her legs to take full advantage of the showcase effect. Her legs were beautifully formed, tightly encased in the sheerest nylons Tommy had ever seen. So sheer, in fact, that he realized abruptly they were more an impression than a certainty. Her knees were smooth, and not all boned—a thing that he thought ruined too many women's otherwise magnificent appendages.

"Excuse me?" Tommy heard himself say.

She smiled a wide, perfect, clear smile that made the tine lines about her blue eyes crinkle. "I saw your shadow fall across the glass, and then you just stood there. I was wondering how long it was going to take you to open the door. Nervous?"

Tommy found himself grinning back at her

weakly. He ran a hand through his hair, shrugged his ex-football player shoulders deprecatingly, and nodded.

She slid back her steno chair and stood up. The burnished tints of her copper hair caught in the desk light's glare, and for an instant Tommy was full to the top with the sight of her; she was easily the most beautiful woman he had ever seen in the flesh. In point of fact...she *looked* familiar, though he was convinced he had never met her before.

"I'll bet you're Mr. Denniss, the writer," she ventured, the smile crossing her face again.

"That's right, but how did you know?"

She breathed deeply—for no apparent reason—and her well-filled sweater swelled alarmingly, causing Tommy's eyes to wander. "Simple. Appointment. You came in at 3:29 exactly," she pointed at the desk clock, "and the book says a Mr. Denniss has an appointment with Mr. Mills at 3:30. Simple?"

"Simple," he agreed. He studied her under cover of a slight cough, and in an instant had cataloged her to memory so he would never forget any part of her. From the top of her copper-colored head, to the line where the desktop cut her legs off from sight.

Wasp-waisted, flair-hipped, full-breasted and a face not idly beautiful like so many girls, but gorgeous with a great many character lines. He classed it at once a "sensitive" face.

"I'll tell Mr. Mills you're here," she said, stepping around the desk.

She walked toward the swinging gate in the

low fence separating the waiting room from the inner offices, apparently to go directly to Mills's office, and Tommy wondered why she was making such an effort: an intercom box stood on the desk.

The reason became quickly apparent. She walked for no one but him. Each step taken as though she walked a terribly thin bridge spanning an abyss. Her feet were placed just so, walking tight and smooth as a panther, with a reserved fire that proved to even the most jaded, that here was an example of the breed *all-woman*. He watched her dutifully, with a dry mouth, aware for the first time in two years that there were things as important as a writing career.

"Say," he stopped her with the word, then realized he *had* wanted to, but had *not* intended to do so, "haven't I seen you somewhere before?"

He added quickly, "And that isn't a pitch I'm making. It's just that, that you look so darned familiar." He had wanted to say *damned familiar*, but somehow it didn't fit in her presence.

Her smile became enigmatic, and she walked back to the desk. From a sheaf of magazines held between bookends, she drew a copy of *Kingpin* and handed it to him. She walked away quickly, letting the gate swing wildly, letting him stand there with the magazine.

Tommy turned it over and saw her on the cover, smiling out at him from a mirror in which she sat combing her hair. The magazine automatically opened to the centerfold, and as the heavy stock paper spread in his hands, he *knew* where he had seen her before.

She had been *Kingpin's* QUEEN OF THE MONTH for October. The spread expanded in front of him, and Tommy Denniss felt very much like the poor Arab boy who had always dreamed of owning a magic lantern and who sees supernatural smoke billowing from the dusty lamp in his hands. There she was, Maxine Rechelle.

He had oo-ed and ah-ed over her picture when he had first seen the issue several months before. It was part of his marketing routine, to read at least three issues of any magazine to which he was submitting to learn their slant and what styles they preferred. But perusing this issue had been much, much more than work. It was recreation of high order.

The picture showed Maxine stretched tight and high, reaching for a jar of marmalade on a kitchen shelf. She was wearing a thigh-length transparent *peignoir*, and as she had stretched for the photo, the nightie had drawn up till it revealed the swell and dip of her buttocks, the dimple on the side to the camera. The thin garment had drifted up and sloped off her high, full breasts with matchless smoothness.

Her hair was long and copper, and her body was sweet as the wind beyond the mountains. He had loved the picture then—in a hopeless, I'll-never-meet-anything-half-that-good fashion—and he loved it even more now in a flickeringly hopeful, by-God-that's-*her*! fashion. He watched the idly swinging gate, and then forcibly shut Maxine from his mind.

He was small potatoes and he knew it; she probably dated dozens of glamorous male models, writers, editors, celebrities, every night. There wasn't a chance for him.

He sighed.

She called, "Mr. Mills will see you now."

She held the gate for him. As he brushed past, she purposely took a step toward him. The tip of her breasts skimmed his jacket, and he suddenly felt as though Dante had inferno-lit his jacket. He gulped audibly, and a tiny chuckle escaped her.

He walked past to the office she indicated, making sure—by dint of real concentration—he did not turn to look at her again. That way led madness.

He knocked on the office door, and a heavy, phlegmy voice boomed, "In, in, in! C'min already, fer Chrissakes!"

Tommy opened the door and was confronted by a bottle of beer. With a human head. It was the most startling analogy he had ever drawn. The man behind the desk was tiny-headed, slim-necked, and huge-bodied. His skin was an uneven dark brown, as though his sun-lamp treatments had been spotty. His hair was bushy and white, and he looked like nothing so much as a bottle of beer with a head of overflowing foam.

"Mr. Mills?" Tommy asked, and the man gestured with short, sharp, impatient motions toward a straight-back chair across from the heavy desk. Tommy sat down nervously, edging about in the chair, crossing, then re-crossing his legs.

"Always like to keep them at attention. No sleepers in *my* crowd. No sir." Mills spoke in staccato roughness.

Tommy looked about in confusion, trying to reconcile the preceding statements with anything at all. Finally, "Pardon?"

Mills gestured at the uncomfortable straight chair. "Straight. Keeps 'em alert. Good for circulation."

He beamed.

Tommy thought ruefully, noticing the plush and stuffed chair in which the beer bottle slumped, *Your circulation must be straight from hunger, if that's true.*

"Now!" caroled Mills. "Denniss. Read your stories."

Tommy beamed back at Gordon Mills. Good news was at hand. The first break.

"Stunk!" Mills finished. He drew the three manuscripts from a basket on the desk labeled "Outgoing" and slapped them down in front of Tommy.

Tommy was crushed. Internally, but not enough to let his fast-fading surface veneer vanish completely. "Stunk? What do you mean? If they stunk…I mean *stink*, why did you call me to come in and see you?"

Mills laid a pudgy finger alongside his fleshy nose. "Ah! That's it. Point of your being here and all. Like the way you write. Good plotting, tight. Fine, deep characterization. Brilliant concepts. Snap endings. Great stuff. Brilliant, brilliant, brilliant!"

He clapped his hands in childlike glee.

Tommy's face read confusion trebled. "But if that's all true...if you're so enthused about my work...why don't you buy them?"

"No good for *Kingpin*. One vital ingredient missing."

Tommy found himself speaking machine-gun fashion, caught up in Mills's style. "What ingredient?"

Mills winked an eye, made a pistol with his thumb and forefinger, aimed at Tommy's cheekbone. "Zilch," he cried.

"Zilch?"

"Ah! Zilch!"

"What's zilch? What zilch?"

"The very foundation of American Man's Everyday life. Ah! Zilch! Can't live without it!"

"Zilch?"

Mills nodded in agreement. Tommy was forced to repeat his question. After Mills had reminded him several times that zilch was everything in stories to be sold to *Kingpin*, Tommy asked again, "But what is it?"

Mills drew a copy of *Kingpin* from the basket marked "Reference" and opened it to a page marked with a paper clip. He indicated several sections heavily boxed in by blue pencil. "Read. Done for us by Helen French. Great guy who wrote this yarn."

Tommy was swimming in a sea of confusion. "But I thought you said Helen French wrote this?"

Mills agreed. "Right. Great guy."

"You mean 'she' is a 'he'? 'He' writes fiction

like a woman would?"

"Naw," Mills countered, "he writes like a dirty broad would, if she was writing like a dirty guy." Mills nodded again, motioned Tommy to read. He read, and this is what he read:

> Stella moaned audibly. Roger pressed tighter against her hot, yielding body. His fierce hands pressed even more tightly to her naked, upthrust breasts, kneading the smoldering tips, like two hot little pencil erasers. The perdition-heat of her fiery little tongue stung him, and with a howl he was upon her and they lay writhed and buffeted and then they ...

Tommy slapped the magazine down quickly, his face white. "P-p-pencil erasers?" he quivered. It had been two years ... no sense getting upset *now*. But the bewilderment, amazement, shock and even horror of what he had read painted his face glaring, garishly.

"Eh? See? Great, isn't it? French is great for zilch. Put his name on the cover, everything. Really sells copies!" Mills was triumphant, crowing, beaming, raving.

Tommy kept shaking his head, as though what he had read was drowning him, filling his nose with some sort of dark effluvium, and he had to swish it clear. As though he was totally confused. His eyes narrowed and his brow furrowed in bewilderment.

This was zilch?

"This is zilch?"

"Ah!" Mills made an unknown conclusion.

"That's it, boy. That's why I called you in here."

Tommy still could not decide what possible connection this—this—*zilch* had to do with him, or his writing. The stories that welled up from within Tommy Denniss had none of this, well, frankly titillating matter in them. He was a *story* writer. Not a purveyor of…of…He suddenly realized he himself had found the paragraph stimulating. He wrenched himself from it mentally, with an effort. He was getting all sorts of gymnastic impressions in his mind, pictured with himself and Maxine Rechelle.

"I don't understand, sir," Tommy threw in, hoping it would clarify Mills's position. Which it did, admirably.

"Your stuff is great, Denniss. Really great. It's a wonder you haven't made a name for yourself already. Can only conclude it's the vagaries of this rotten business that've held you back. How long have you been writing? Well, anyhow," he did not pause to let Tommy answer, "what I want from you is some zilch stories, boy. Need 'em bad. Always need 'em. I can buy three-four-maybe-even-five a month from you, if you can turn 'em out."

Tommy was, in the main, flabbergasted. Him turn out zilch? Stories like—like *that*? He was first appalled, then frightened. Here was a chance to break in, but he wasn't sure he wanted it. Would he be prostituting—literally—his talent? He shrugged away *that* objection; he was no Sartre or Hemingway, and he knew it; he was a storyteller with talent, and that was about all; if he could write *good* zilch, why not? But *could* he write good zilch? Could he write it at all? The very thought brought a red flush to his cheeks. He knew he had a deep-seated Puritan streak somewhere near his streak of lechery, but would it keep him from writing good zilch?

"I'm not sure I can write this kind of stuff," he put his thoughts into words. Mills waved away the objection.

"Boy, we've got a system around here. We've got a brand-new kind of fiction here. Zilch is a new kind of writing." Tommy wasn't so sure about *that* as he recalled the Decameron and Balzac and P'u Sung-ling. "We have to create a new kind of writer. There's a cultural *need* for this sort of stuff, lad."

He seemed bent upon a familiar lecture dealing with the insecurity of the modern American male, his repressions, psychoses, fetishes and mental/physical habits. Tommy listened with growing amazement, disbelief, and confusion.

Finally, he shook his head. "No, I—I don't think I can do that sort of stuff. You see, my stories all…"

Mills broke in. "Our system, boy. *Great* system. Here take a batch of these *Kingpins*. Read 'em. Study 'em. Then do us a few stories. Three hundred dollars each."

Tommy grabbed for the magazines. The sum of three hundred per was too much to resist. He had the magazines, and then he was thanking Mills, and a few moments later he was bolting to the elevator.

Not till he was on the first floor, did he realize

he had passed Maxine Rechelle without a word. And her sitting there so beautiful, her mouth smiling, her chest jutting, and her legs framed in the desk hole with the skirt hiked *awfully* high.

He kicked himself mentally, but decided not to let himself worry about it. He was going to be back soon, very soon. And then he might strike up a conversation with her.

Maybe.

Mills read the three stories while Tommy waited, and after each one, his face grew tighter and tighter, and more unhappy. At last he turned over the final page, tamped the sheaf together and put the paper clip back on it. He shook his head of foam, and his little watery brown eyes were terribly sad.

"Boy, I *know* you've got the stuff in you. These stories are great! Really great!" Tommy thrilled.

"But they're no good," Mills finished.

Tommy flattened.

"They're fine stuff, son, but just not zilch. There's none of that—uh—*feeling*, what I mean. Here, I've got an idea. Maxine, our receptionist. She's written a few of these for us under a pseudonym. Got the right feeling there, that girl. Real hot stuff. The stories, that is. She's the one to help you on this, boy. I've got my sights set. Gonna make you the biggest name in zilch. Fame. Fortune. Alla *that* hokum."

He stabbed at the intercom, and Tommy half-rose from the seat, to stop him. No, no! Anything but Maxine Rechelle. She was the *last* person he wanted to help him write zilch. It had been hard enough writing the stories as it was—sweating and licking his lips—and he had failed even then. How would it be with a magnificent piece of flesh like her on the job? He shuddered deliciously inside, and damned the day he submitted to *Kingpin*.

"Maxine. C'min."

Mills clicked the intercom, and sat back with a smug grin. "She'll do it, boy. That girl knows what's what."

Maxine came through the door, the dress molded to every luscious line of her, from V to breasts, and back again. His mouth dried away to dust, and he shut his eyes very tight.

From somewhere far away he heard Maxine's satin-over-velvet voice insinuatingly saying, "Why, certainly, Mr. Mills. I'll be only too happy to help Mr. Denniss out with his zilch."

God spare me in my hour of need, Tommy Denniss thought to himself, floating at ten thousand feet on a jet-propelled cotton candy cloud of light blue.

"Tommy, honey," Maxine said, curling her shoeless feet beneath her skirt, where she curled up on the couch. "Now I want you to understand I have no personal interest in you." Her apartment was semi-plush and throbbed with the muted strains of Rachmaninoff's Second Concerto. "What I'm going to try and teach you—actually, just make you *aware* of— about zilch, is strictly business. You understand that, don't you?"

Tommy nodded numbly. Somehow, he had gotten from the offices, all the way across town, and here to Maxine's apartment, without so much as taking two breaths. He was ready to swear to that! The nearness of her was so acute, he felt a queasy pain in his solar plexus. He had never been so close to so much beauty in all his life.

"Fine," she beamed. She patted the couch beside her. Tommy got the message and walked across to her slowly; he sat down with difficulty, turning half away to save embarrassment. "Now don't dare forget," she admonished him, "think of all this research in the context of story."

She was studying his roughly handsome face with something more than clinical interest, and her eyes went across his ex-football player's body with open wonder.

Then she was very close to him, and her body was pressed very tight. He could feel the ribbing of her bra, and the wrinkles of her slip, even through his shirt. He tried to think of all this in the context of story.

The girl smothered his face with her hands, he thought wildly, trying to keep fact separated from fiction. *Her face was hot, and her hands were live things that moved across his body. He responded at first slowly, then more quickly, as he felt the blood in himself churning.*

Her back was smooth, and he ran his hands up that back, he thought, doing it.

Then Tommy's mind faltered in its track of narrative, and he knew he was lost for the moment. There was going to be no clinical interest, as she stripped away his clothes. There was going to be no cold setting-down of what was happening, to transcribe in story form, as he peeled away her sweat-soaked undergarments.

There was going to be nothing now, as their bodies met, but the fury of the moment.

Undoubtedly later it would be burned into his loins and mind, but now, right now...

Mills laid the eighth of the eight stories aside. His brown face was coated with perspiration. He looked across the desk at Tommy Denniss with open amazement, a shock of fright visible, also. His mouth worked loosely, and his hands strove to find something.

"They're—they're...unbelievable!" he murmured in awe.

Tommy was exultant. It had been an ordeal. A heavenly ordeal, but a real struggle nonetheless. He had written the eight stories the same night. One right after the other, till the next night had come, and he had spent *more* time with Maxine. They were the finest zilch ever written. No doubt about that!

He was slightly worried, for the hot streak of writing had glowed within him, he tried to write a non-zilch piece, just to keep his hand in. He had found himself unable to do it. He could write nothing *but* zilch now, it seemed.

But it didn't bother him. Zilch was the greatest thing since the invention of the padded brassiere. He was going to be rolling in money, and that would keep Maxine happy, for he knew now that he was ensnared. She was a fierce woman, with the most volcanic demands he'd ever imagined, and it would take a lot of money to keep her interested in him, no matter *how* broad his shoulders were.

But there was no doubt on that score. Mills obviously thought the pieces were brilliant. At $300 a story, that was two thousand, four hundred dollars. Wow!

Mills reached into his desk, drew out a slip of paper, and attached it by a paper clip to the top of the stack of stories. *Ah, a voucher for the money!* Tommy chuckled within.

Mills was pale beneath his imperfect tan.

"We can't publish these," he breathed in fright. "The damed things would get us booted off the newsstands in a second. Don't know where you got this kind of material, boy. But lay off it. You'll never sell it. Too damned—too damned—well, too *zilchy!*"

He shook his head in finality, rose and left the office, having laid the sheaf of manuscripts before Tommy Denniss. Tommy stared down at the slip of paper clipped to them, and realized his troubles were just beginning. What with Maxine's demands of the flesh, and the pocketbook, and his inability to let her go now, having sampled her fruits—not to mention his total inability to write anything *but* zilch—he was doomed.

He stared silently, with a sinking but growing horror, at the slip of paper.

Brother, were his troubles just beginning:

The little slip of paper, neatly printed, the first of many such to say, very definitely:

REJECTED.

God Bless the Ugly Virgin

WHEN A PERSON IS TWENTY-SEVEN years old (as Katy Pascal was) and she knows she is quite homely (as Katy Pascal was), but she knows she has a fantastically proportioned body (as Katy Pascal had), and still she's a virgin (as Katy Pascal most assuredly was), a person begins to get restless.

Katy Pascal had been restless for ten years.

In fact, it might be said that her restlessness had slowly but steadily turned into a form of "animal-pacing-cage" tension. She had a habit of wetting her lips, licking her chops, when a handsome man walked past her at the lunch counter in Clancy's Diner.

Katy would study herself for hours at a time, in the full-length mirror of her two-room apartment. She knew it was a form of narcissism and that many people would consider her strange, but she *had* to reassure herself constantly that the body was magnificent enough to offset the face. Because the face was ghastly.

She would stand tip-toe before the mirror, stretching lithely toward the ceiling, after her shower, rubbed pink and smooth by a fluffy bath towel. She would watch the muscles tighten, and the ridges stand out down her chest, and the hollows appear in her buttocks, and the straining eagerness of fresh, untouched flesh.

She would raise up till her stomach lost its incipient tiny bulge, and hollowed in, sweeping up to magnificent rose-tipped breasts and sweeping down to rich, full thighs. Breasts that were not too large, but which angled softly upward near their tips, pointing off away from her, into the sky.

Breasts that she cupped with hot hands, feeling the giving smoothness of them, the fiery pulsing of blood in them. That she wanted to press so *desperately* against a man's chest.

Thighs that were round and unblemished, marked by the indentations of her stocking tops. Cream-colored and firm, long and rewarding. Thighs that ached to be pressed around some man's body.

Her eyes were brown, and her hair was a gleaming chestnut color, hanging pageboy to her shoulders with glosses and shimmers.

The body was magnificent—but the face was a nightmare.

Her body was delicate, with a voluptuousness that came from ample proportions without overabundance. But her face was someone else's face; it was heavy, massive, almost lantern-jawed. The chin was cleft, the nose was angled, the cheekbones far too prominent. Her teeth protruded slightly, and that compounded with the granite, jutting jaw to give a decidedly prognathous appearance to an otherwise dazzling form.

Singly, most of the mismatched features of her face might not have been unpleasant, might even have been attractive. But combined, they were fearsome, and Katy had gone twenty-seven innings without a hit.

She had finally decided to score…since Luck seemed to already to have thrown the game.

She had waited, and watched, and selected in her own mind, only coming to the decision after deep inner struggles. She wouldn't hope for marriage any longer—hat was out of the question—but she would do away with this damnable virgin state, at once. She was going to seduce a man! After she watched and waited and selected, she decided on a calculated plan of action, and the objective was Milt Rodman.

Milt Rodman who drove truck over-Turnpike between New York and Cleveland, carting fresh fruit for A&P. Milt Rodman who stopped in Clancy's Diner where she worked for a steak (medium-rare), French fries (well-done) and apple pie (a piece of cheese on top, please) when going either way.

Katy would have liked to think that Milt stopped to see her, but that wasn't the case. The case was simple enough. Clancy's food was good.

But once Katy had mentally winnowed through all the hundreds of men who stopped in at the Diner, she settled on Milt. It took a while to decide, but finally she knew it was him, because of the hesitancy with which he talked about his conquests to the other truckers. They all bellowed and winked lecherously, and swore, telling about the broads they'd layed, but Milt always spoke in softer tones, telling the stories he infrequently told, with a certain restraint and obvious gentlemanly regard for the girls concerned. That was the kind of man she wanted to seduce her!

Big Milt, with shoulders like a Chinese water-carrier (the ones with the big stick across their shoulders), and a face like the truck had run over his kisser while he was down underneath repairing a flat. Big Milt with the big hands, and the slow tongue … and the hot eyes.

He had never said anything more to Katy than his order, might not really have seen her. It was like that with most of the men. But she stood by the grill and watched him when he was stopping in. Watched how the muscles bunched against his shirt, how the sweat stood out on his neck and forehead. She watched the tightness of his pants about his hips, and she dreamed at night of that body pressed on top of hers, his big, heavy hands exploring every crevice, every dark shape of her body, and she tossed terribly on her bed, biting the back of her hand, and swearing she would get to Milt Rodman.

Because Katy Pascal had decided to give him her virginity.

It was difficult getting Milt into a compromising position. Very difficult, because once she had decided it would be Milt, she wanted no one else. And it struck her as strange she *was* a virgin. Many times she had heard the truckers on the lunch stools say:

"I don't give a damn *how* ugly a dame is, Willie, there's always bound to be at least *one* guy that's an opportunist, or on the make and desperate enough to take one around the block!"

Then they would re-order, laughing lewdly about how they'd lay any broad inna world no matter how ugly she was, just so long as she was available. Then they would re-order—looking right through her as she winked back at them availably.

And if that was so—that any girl who wanted to be made *would* be made, just by the laws of inevitability—why the hell *was* she still unexploited territory?

The problem got more acute as she started her plan to make Milt aware of her, to throw herself at him. She had her hair done, with a henna rinse, with little flecks of gold dancing in it, and she wore it upswept. She wore her oldest uniforms that weren't faded, the tightest ones; and she hip-swished around Milt, eyeing him openly, licking her lips till they glistened, stopping just in sight of him by the curve of the counter and slowly pulling up her skirt, up the long, lithe length of her leg, and tightening her garters right before him. She didn't clean off the counter before him from her proper place in front of him, but came around, out into the lunchroom, and leaned over his shoulder to wipe the rag around the formica. Brushing his back and arms and sides with her hot, tensed, straining breasts.

And because of this, the problem got much worse, more acute. Because at that point the *other* truckers seemed to realize she was radiating a sex-aura, seemed to realize she *was* a woman, and that she *was* on the make. And they decided: *Ugly? So what? Put a bag over her face, etc., etc.*

It seemed that the moment Katy became aware of her womanhood—perhaps not her *desirable* womanhood, but the basic fact of femininity itself—she began to exude some wonderful something that made the other truckers look at her with a new light in their eyes. But she knew what that light was. They still thought she was ugly, but man, she was available...and such a dog they could get her anytime! That's what they thought.

Katy thought that was it, which it was of course, and since their interest was strictly carnal, she rejected them mentally, one by one.

Until only Milt Rodman was left. He was virile, and he looked so damned...so damned...she couldn't quite think of the proper word. But he didn't ogle her and make lecherous tooth-sucking noises when she passed. He talked big like the rest of them in their stool bull-sessions, but he seemed more of a gentleman. Perhaps more shy, but still hot-eyed, and...and...*what* was the word?

So Katy laid on the charm double-thick when he breezed in. She leaned over the counter, shoving her well-made breasts practically into his face. The hello she gave him was extra warm, the meat she cut him was extra rare, the cut of pie she served him was extra large.

Yet Milt never seemed to notice.

Three months went quickly by, with Katy getting more frantic. She had decided on a man finally, and he might move to a new route without noticing her. Then she would sink back into that single, lethargic, doomed state of ugly virginity.

She tried everything but tripping him and carting him off unconscious.

Finally, she hit upon a scheme that was bound to work, by its very blatancy. Even though Milt always came into the Diner, sat down and ate, gabbed a bit with the other boys off-duty, paid, got up and left ... she was certain the plan would succeed. He acted as though he was in a trance, as far as she was concerned, and she decided it was probably because he could have a hundred pretty girls, so why should he bother with her. He watched his plate when he ate, and when he *did* look up, it was usually to locate the ketchup.

Which was usually centered directly between Katy's breasts.

But the plan was bound to work ... she took a week just to work it out perfectly.

Thursday night, late, as Milt was finishing his dinner, prepared to sack-in on the front seat of the truck preparatory to the long drive into New York in the morning to catch the wholesale markets, Katy sidled up to him. She leaned in toward him, breathing her perfume delicately at his face.

The other truckers stopped eating and seeing her hip-movement, began staring surreptitiously.

In a low, throaty voice she had been practicing all week, Katy mellowed, "Hi, Milt."

The big, chunky-faced man looked up, surprise dotting his eyes, a certain cornered look there. It seemed for the first time in his life he had heard this woman speak, but he tossed it off quickly and grinned broadly, "Uh, yeah... baby? What kin I do fer ya?"

A roguish grin lit his face, and the other truckers chuckled in secret knowledge.

"Milt, will you give me a hand tonight?"

"Uh, how ya mean?"

"Well, I've got a big load of packages in the back, and I was hopin' I'd find somebody to help me carry them home."

Milt looked dubious for a moment, began to say something, but Katy hurriedly added, "I'm not kiddin', Milt. I really need somebody's help. My apartment's onny a couple blocks, and it'll onny take a few minutes."

Slowly, like some gigantic machine grounding weightily to the end of its cycle, Milt stared at her with decision forming.

Oh, migod, he's starin' at me so close, thought Katy in wildness. *Don't let him think I'm too ugly for a fast one. Please don't let him!*

Milt's expression changed. He nodded his head, "Okay, I'll help ya," and he went back to his veal chops.

Katy was abruptly covered in goose-pimples, now that the time was so near. She quickly left the lunchroom and went to the kitchen, where she persuaded the diminutive Clancy to get the relief girl in to replace her... right now! Then she changed into her street dress, and gathered up all the heavy packages of boxes she had loaded with sand, bricks and rocks, that afternoon.

Just as she re-emerged into the lunchroom,

she heard Milt talking with three of the truckers. A florid-faced man who had whistled at her several time was saying gaily, "Well, I knew that poot would come across one day. Now that you got the ice broke, we can all expect to get it reg'lar."

He was grinning, even as Milt shoved him hard against the cigarette machine.

"Watch ya goddam mouth, ya stupid slob!" Milt was angry, and Katy felt a swelling of pride. And an aching in her loins at the same moment. He had stood up for her!

"Shall we go, Milt," she interrupted, before the fight could progress any further. They left together, Milt carrying the dummy packages, and Katy added an extra hip-swish just to make those stupid truckies jealous.

Once in the apartment, it wasn't difficult to get Milt to stay.

"Would you like a drink, Milt?"

She carefully dropped the packages she had taken from Milt on the only available chair in the living room, indicating he should sit down on the sofa.

"Uh, yeah, that's swell," he answered nervously. "What'cha got...baby?"

"You name it," she said, moving closer, till she was looking up into his ruggedly sprawling features. She didn't know where she had acquired this coquettishness, but now that she needed it, here it was. Her voice had sunk to a deeper key, and Milt looked down at her, half-brazenly, half-uncertainly.

He looked so...so...she fumbled with the word, caught by the bright shine of Milt's eyes on her body, and finally came up with the right one. *Competent.* He looked damned *competent.*

"Uh, maybe I better not, uh, have that drink after all, ba...Katy. I, uh, gotta, uh, go back to the truck to sack out, ya know. I got that, uh, trip into the city tomorrow mornin'."

Katy moved toward him carefully, letting her hands slide up his chest till they rested on his shoulders. "I've got an idea, Milt," she said huskily. "Why don'tcha sleep here tonight and go back to your truck in the mornin'. It's much more...comfortable here."

Milt backed away, but she stayed with him.

This ain't no way for a red-hot competent man to act, Katy's thought bombarded her.

"No...I...uh...y'see, the truck's back there on the lot at Clanc..."

"It's locked, isn't it?" she asked coyly.

"Well, yeah, *sure* it's locked, but I gotta—"

She moved closer again, touching him lightly, as though she were handling a hot pan. She didn't know where these movements were coming from, how she knew the right thing, the stimulating thing, to do—but suddenly she wasn't thinking, just letting her body and her emotions lead her.

"Welllll then..." and she let it trail off slightly, letting her tongue glide smoothly, moistly, over her full lips.

She backed him another inch, and he collided with the sofa, sitting himself down heavily. To Katy he seemed to be looking about wildly, and she was vaguely glad to be between him and the door.

With a sinuous movement Katy slid down next to him, letting her high heels slip off, and folding her long legs beneath her. In the same motion she flicked off the lamp near the sofa. The room was now lit by only one dim bulb in the torchier near the television set.

As though drawing attention to the seclusion of the setting, Katy ventured, "We can watch a good show, and have a few drinks, and then maybe, well…" she trailed off again. Strange how effective *not* saying something could be.

Then, almost before she knew she was doing it, she was leaning forward, and her hands slid over his shoulders, down his broad back, and she was so close she could feel her breasts being smoothed flat in their bra casings, and even crouching on the sofa that way, she was close to him—all the way from her stomach to her lips. Which were on his own.

Hers were soft and pliant, while Milt's were thick and chapped. But somehow that made her all the more boiling inside, all the more anxious to have him, to let him take her. She let her tongue slide from her mouth , and met the slightly giving surface of his lips. Her tongue worked itself, trying to open his mouth, and like a bomb going off in her vitals, deeper than any physician might probe, her body prickled and burned, and she rubbed herself fiercely on him, till her whole being was a writhing thing demanding satiation.

His lips remained closed, and for an instant

she brought her tongue back... then struck suddenly!

His mouth opened to hers, and the warmth of their bodies met in the mingled moisture of the kiss. She arched herself forward, feeling her nipples harden and press toward him. God, how she wanted to rip off her dress!

Then, as though it had been a signal, Milt himself began to move, pressing his heavy legs toward hers, and in a moment they had twisted—awkwardly but swiftly—and he was lying on her, his weight a great thing pressing her down.

She moved her own legs with difficulty, letting them slide open slowly, letting his weight settle down on her even farther. Letting the heat of his loins reach her own.

His hands suddenly left her hips, began moving up and down, the skirt rising, the buttons seeming to open on the dress front of their own accord. Then she felt the heat of his questing fingers, all along her thighs, and a tremor ran through her body. She felt his hands touching, touching, touching, on the inside of her legs, on her stomach, in the hollow of her torso, and then he was maneuvering away the fabric of the restricting bra, his fingers digging themselves with wonderful pain into the soft, firm flesh of her breasts. She had *known* he would be competent!

He settled back for an instant, as though about to commence a new attack on her yielding body, and his mouth moved off hers for a split second.

"Wait a minute…Milt…wait…a…" she breathed out in a gasp, as he settled away from her. "Lemme get this dress off, it's my best one, and I don't wanna rip it, y'know."

Abruptly, he was off her, and moving toward the door, his steps faltering and shambling, as though he were drunk with some particularly heady wine.

Katy sat up on the sofa, her breath coming shortly, her dress tight around her thighs, the smooth roll of her stocking tops making indentations in the firm flesh of her legs. One of her garters had come unfastened, and her brown hair was all about her face. She stared at him in bewilderment, then leaped up and grabbed his arm before he could twist the doorknob.

"Where ya goin'? Huh, where ya goin', Milt?"

He stared at her, and there was sweat on his face. His roughly heavy features were twisted in misery, but he let one corner of his mouth quiver up into a smile of mock bravado.

"I-I gotta, uh, go, baby. You know how it is, uh, Katy."

"Oh no y'don't!" she yelled, almost angrily, and grabbed him by the arm with both hands. She dragged him back toward the sofa with one step. And suddenly, summoning strength from some deep pit of emotion, she swung him full-force, tossing him back on the sofa. "You siddown again!"

She stood over him with hands on her hips, her hair disarrayed, her dress rumpled and still hiked tight to her full hips.

"Look, Katy…y'gotta unnerstan'…I, uh, you

gotta let me tell ya something..."

A look of strained bewilderment came across Katy Pascal's twenty-seven year old virgin features, and she sat down beside him. "Tell me *what*?"

"I...I...well, see my Mom, she... oh, no, I *can't* tell ya!"

Katy slapped her forehead with the palm of her hand, and almost cried in hysteria. "Can't *tell* me? Can't *tell* me? Jeezus, Gawd! I practically *throw* myself at ya, and ya try to walk out on me! Then ya tell me ya can't *tell* me! I know I ain't no Kim Novak, but..."

Milt quickly turned to her, pain rising in his face.

"No sir, baby!" he said definitely and with assurance, almost belligerently, as though she were castigating herself unnecessarily, "that ain't it at all. It's not that you're ugly...*uh!*" He looked as though he had fallen into a barrel of pig manure as the word "ugly" left his lips. He covered it quickly but stumblingly with, "I mean, cause you ain't as good-lookin' as some. It, uh, ain't, uh, that at all."

Katy felt the blood pounding in her ears. She was getting sore.

"Well, then, ya big stupe, what *is* it?"

"Well..." his face suddenly suffused with red, starting from the open neck of his shirt, and climbing like a storm warning to the roots of his hair. He was blushing, and Katy felt herself melting inside. The big, overgrown...

"Go on," Katy urged more softly, moving closer, till her thigh touched his. She wanted to begin that animal rubbing again, but held off for fear it might ruin Milt's explanation. *But this ain't no way for a* competent *man to act,* she thought wryly.

"Well, y'see, I'm thirty-two, and I been livin' with my Mom all that time, and she...well...oh, heck!" He started to rise again, stopped cold in his track of thought, but Katy yanked roughly and he plopped down again. She prodded him.

"Go on. Go on!"

Milt's words abruptly came spilling out on top of one another. The explanation spewed forth all at once. "My Mom told me never to have anything to do with girls cause they was dirty, and that if I did any of that sexy stuff, I'd come down with the gleep or somethin' and that's why I didn't wanna insult ya because you prob'ly heard me bulling with the other fellas, about all the girls I'd had, and I've never had any, cause actually I'm a...I'm a...virgin, see, and I been watchin' ya for weeks now and I kinda just didn't know how to say hello to ya and I remembered what my Mom said and I can't stay here no more cause if I do I'll prob'ly do some of that sexy stuff with you and then I'll come down with the gleep or somethin' and I'll miss my drive inta the city tomorra'..."

He ran out of air, and slumped back on the sofa dejectedly.

Katy sat wide-eyed. She could still hear his speech, spattering around inside her head. *Competent! Virgin!* Then she began to laugh.

Loud and long, till she was clutching the rumpled sides of her dress, pressing her hands frantically into her firm breasts to stop the laughter-pains. But it was no use.

"Now, uh, baby..." And Katy laughed all the harder, because she realized now why Milt always sounded so self-conscious about using that word. "...don't you laugh at me. C'mon! Stop that. My Mom was right about girls like you...you all got so much, uh, well, so much *experience,* a fella hasn't got a chance; he could get somethin' real bad!"

He seemed so childishly intense, Katy found herself laughing all the more. *Experience?* Oh, Good Gravy, this was *too* much! She roared, even knowing she was hurting him, but she couldn't stop. She tried to get the words out, tried to tell the big, hulking truckdriver *she* was a virgin, too, but they wouldn't come out. They bubbled up in her throat and came out as laughter.

"Now look, don't you be laughin' at me. I didn't mean to say nothin' funny, and if I'd knowed you was gonna laugh, I wouldn't have told ya at all. I didn't mean ta be rude, and if I was gonna do them kinda things with *anybody,* why I'd be pleased to do 'em with you, but my Mom told me..."

Then Katy moved in on him, pressing him back and back and back till he was in the bedroom, and she put herself against the door, and locked it, and let the key fall to the floor, where she kicked it under the radiator, and then she began to undress, while Milt just watched.

She unbuttoned the dress down the front and slipped it over her head, letting it whisper to the floor. Then she reached behind herself, arching her back, and unfastened the bra strap. At that point the dullness left Milt's eyes, and he began undressing, slowly, as though not quite certain what he was doing. He stood there in his shorts and T-shirt, staring at Katy as she moved carefully and sinuously, dropping her panties, rolling down her stockings, moving toward him.

Then she was helping him with the rest of his clothing, and then the cool bed received them, and Milt found the strength to protest, in a small voice, "But my Mom said ... "

And then Katy's lips silenced Milt's Mom's words of warning.

It had been difficult for Katy. There had been some bleeding, but when it was all over, she knew it had been worth it. It had been worth waiting twenty-seven years to enjoy. Even through all his clumsiness and bigness, Milt *had* been competent.

Finally, when the sun streamed through the venetian blinds, and neither of them had slept a wink, Milt got up and took a shower and dressed. Katy lay in bed and watched his big body moving back and forth across the bedroom, and she felt a sorrow building in her.

The big oaf would be gone, and she knew somehow that this was the first and last time she would know that pleasure.

Milt went into the living room, and she heard the front door open. She turned quickly and buried her face in the pillow, the tears mounting to her eyes, and a tightness in her throat. *Hell, not even a little goodbye.*

Then she heard, "Uh…" and turned back to see Milt framed in the doorway.

"I, uh, just wanted to ask if you'd be here tomorrow when I, uh, come back through?"

She smiled and nodded her head yes.

"Well, I'll, uh, help ya carry some more packages if ya need the help. And, uh, maybe we can have another, uh, drink, huh?"

Katy bobbed her head. Then Milt turned to go. He took a step and stopped. He turned, blushing fiercely, and mumbled, "Y'know, you're awful pretty, Katy…baby."

Then he was gone, and Katy lay there figuring.

Milt passed through four times a week.

And that was two hundred and eight times a year.

A Blue Note for Bayou Betty

(as by "Derry Tiger")

HE WAS A TALL, GOOD-LOOKING BOY, with a shock of straw-colored hair that had an odd, copper tone under the sheen of the bandstand lights. Under the blue and green and gold gels his hair seemed rainbowed. And as the lights played across his angular, narrow face, his eyes closed slowly, and he sucked on the end of his cornet with gigantic concentration.

She watched him, hungrily.

She was a cat. The hunger was in her full, red lips, in her dark skin, in the supple lines of her lush body and the high proud awareness of her breasts. She wore a black sheath with rhinestone-studded straps that went over her bare shoulders, and somehow, it was more a skin than a dress.

She watched him with eyes slitted down to green fires, banked tightly, while he moaned his blues for the midnight crowd.

The cornetist's name was Raymond Shamley, and his group was Ray Shamley's Hot Six. Behind him sat five men who played along languidly, allowing the horn to set its own pace. The piano was a fat, little man they called The Dome. He was bald, and his fingers seemed to be boneless, but his music was good, and never intrusive.

The bass and clarinet were brothers:

Tweedledum and Tweedledee. That wasn't their real names. But Dum was da-da-dum on the bass with thick, wide black hands and dee-dee-diddle-dee was his brother Dee on the stick, with sweetnesses trilling and riding when the call came clearly.

Trumpet was an old man they knew only as B.J.

That was all that was needed. B.J. was good enough, because his sounds presented their calling cards.

Cork-In-Water Weist was the drummer. He was a young kid with much oo-chack-boom in his good strong left, and sti-pa-sti-pa-stititititi-pa in his radamacue right. None of them were great, but all of them bore the seeds of great, and all of them loved Ray Shamley, and all of them together made something not one of them could make.

Together there was cool of a high order.

Hot and cool, so fast and so sweet and so deep…

She watched him, while he swung out and rode his blues till they hurt everyone down here, down where they thought private, dark things. And *she* dug, and *she* thought: this is the guy for me. This is the guy I want, and the guy who can do the trick for me, who'll do it for me, for my beautiful, hot body. This is the guy who'll kill my fat, ugly husband.

While he gave his sounds to the world.

Ray Shamley slept in loud pajamas.

He was a good kid, just twenty-seven, rangy

and clean-looking, who strangely enough, had never known a woman. It was not that he had no desire, it was simply he had been too busy making something of himself. He had been devoted to his cornet, and to the truth it told, and there had never really been time for a clean kid from a good home to find the sort of women who hung around jazzmen. He had been too busy.

He slept in loud pajamas. It was a foible.

There was a knock on his hotel room door. He let his dark eyes narrow, and the cigarette between his lips freed a heavy filigree of smoke that rose to the low ceiling and the water pipes.

"Yeah?" he challenged the closed door.

"Mr. Shamley?" A voice that was all muffledness and deep came back at him.

"Yeah. Who's that?"

"I'd like to speak with you, if you've got a minute?" the woman's voice asked, and there was a tone under the overtone.

"Wait a minute," he said, reaching for the robe across the foot of the bed. The slippers were on the other side of the bed, and he didn't like the damn things anyway, so he belted the robe tightly and padded to the door barefoot.

Gracefully she stood there, as though poised to leap. He took her in, from the head of tightly-curled short ebony hair, down across the full, bloody lips and the white rise of her throat, to the sharp, high mounds of her breasts, squeezed in their half-bra cups till they rose up from the bodice of the sheath with impatience.

"What, uh, what can I do for you?" his mouth

was filled with a soft, blue dust.

"My name is Betty. My friends call me Bayou Betty. I'm from N'wawlens—" was the way she said it, "—and if you've got a minute or two, I'd like to—talk—to you."

She said *talk*, but talk wasn't what she wanted.

"Well, sure," he moved aside, "c'mon in. Like a drink?"

Ray Shamley was about to become a man.

She took him like Attila took Asia. By storm, by conquest, by brutality. She descended on him and used him, and he was whipped like a dog.

To hell with preliminaries, was her method. She gained access to the room, and asked him for music, and he turned on the room's wall radio and it played softly some anonymous music, and she danced with him, pressing her fleshy body into his.

She used her hips, grinding them tightly against him, so that he felt her fire within his pajamas, felt the burning heat of her thighs and her stomach against his own. She made some minor reference to having seen him every night in the club, of having wanted him for a very long time, but it didn't matter.

And when she stopped dancing and kissed him with her mouth and her teeth and her tongue, so that his head swam, there was no need for pretence. His hands went into her flesh ruggedly, and she gasped as she pressed to him.

"Wait...wait a minute..." she managed to moan, and twisted free of him, to taunt him a bit more.

He stood watching her as she reached behind herself; he heard a zipper, and her hands went to the straps over her shoulders. A shrug, and she was free of the clinging black sheath. It lay in a silken puddle around her feet, and she watched his eyes as he took in the sight of her in bra and pants and hose.

The music still curled from the wall radio, and she moved almost in rhythm to it. She reached behind her and unsnapped the brassiere. She held it away from her, in an outstretched hand, and Ray Shamley's breath caught in his chest at the sight of her breasts.

They were full, and when she removed the encircling bra they did not fall. Coral-tipped and pointed toward heaven.

She dropped the bra and began to roll down the light blue pants. The elastic rolled tightly, hugging her hips, till the fabric was a thin roll across her thighs. With a fluid movement she stripped the pants down, and was standing completely naked.

Her arms went up and opened, and Ray Shamley grabbed her tightly, by the hair, pulling her face to his. His lips were cruel on hers, and she bit his tongue with gentle ferocity. Their bodies ground together, and he forced her back back back till her knees struck the bed, and they fell atop one another.

Then his hands were on her warm breasts, squeezing the hard, nubbin-like nipples. She moaned softly into his ear, and he felt a moist wind and she blew passionately into it. His hands moved down the length of her body, and locked at her thighs. The dark mat of her womanhood arched up at him as she demanded he take her...violently.

Without volition, he threw off the robe and pajamas and bent to her again. She moved her legs, and for an instant he looked into her cat's eyes, seeing nothing he did not like.

But her arms went around his neck and she drew him down till her breasts pressed tightly against him. Then there was a moment of fumbling—during which she helped him— and then the fiery, yielding oneness of her acceptance.

She made a series of clipped animal whines, and then he struck fully, powerfully; and their bodies clashed in a hell of fury and sensuality.

All through it, while his eyes were closed— from passion and inexperience—she watched him with the eyes of a bayou cat. And she thought: this man will do the job. He'll be the one to kill Ernie, fat, ugly Ernie.

Afterward, he slept. She watched, but he slept.

"How long have I been seeing you, Ray?" she asked.

Three months. He knew how long it was. She was his music now. His blood. His liver, his eyes, his heartbeat. She was in him, of him, all that was him. "Going on three months now, I guess. Why?"

"Ray, would you like us to be together all the time? I mean, permanently?"

He stared at her across the bed. "What do you mean? I thought we *were*—"

"Grow up, Ray! Things aren't always as simple as they look. I'm a married woman."

He was stunned only for an instant. A few months before he would have blushed, and been unable to reconcile it with his upbringing. But she had done her work. She had taken him by storm, and she had broken down his barriers. Now he just stared at her, unspeaking.

Then: "What am *I* supposed to do about it?"

She looked at him with feline intensity. She slid across the passion-damp sheets till her fiery body was pressed to his. She took his head and bent it down to her breasts, and whispered in his ear.

"My husband is a wealthy man, Ray. A very wealthy man. A planter. But he's a slob; ugly, and greasy fat, nothing like you...and he's stupid. I want *you*, Ray. I want you..."

"Well, you can divorce hi—"

"Don't be a *fool!*" she leaped back, thrusting him away venomously. "I want him *dead*, not divorced!"

Ray Shamley sat up and saw her, clearly, for the first time. "You're out of your mind," he managed to gasp.

She came coolly close again, sensing his withdrawal. "Ray, Ray, honey," she ran her hands over him, making him jump with electric shock, "how many times have you told me you want to start a band of your own, not just this cornball combo? How many times have you said you wanted to get out of Louisiana, go to New

York or Chicago?"

"Well, sure I do, but murd—"

"Don't say it like that," she stopped him with a finger to his lips. The odor of her was musky and heady, the smell of woman. "Call it our freedom, honey. We can be together. He's very wealthy, and with all his money, we can go away together…you can become famous."

"Oh, hell! But this is killing!"

"Listen, Ray…"

It took many hours, but there was passion in those hours, and Bayou Betty knew her body, knew her men, and she knew what the answer would finally be.

She introduced Ray to Ernie. She made it seem he was a talented young musician that Ernie should take an interest in furthering. Ray and Ernie spent time together, and Betty had it planned just that way; there would be a time when fat, warty Ernie would have to invite Ray to stay the night. A night when a burglar would invade their big house on the edge of the plantation and kill Ernie with an unlicensed Beretta.

So Ray got to know Ernie.

Finally, the night arrived, and Betty stole into Ray's guest room. She wore a gossamer-thin nightgown, and in the moonlight from the window, every line of her lush, young body stood out in clear sharpness. She came to him, and put his hand under the nightgown. His fingers pressed silken wisps of curliness, and she gasped as she told him: "Fifteen minutes.

I'll be in bed with him. After you do it, we'll break a window on the main floor, and make it look as though a burglar was here. The servants have been given the night off.

"You aren't afraid are you?"

He shook his head, and she reached down to wind her long nails in his hair. She kissed him frantically, ferociously, her mouth open and moist.

Then she slipped the little Italian gun to him.

"Soon," she said.

"Soon," he echoed, and she slipped back to her own bedroom, to the arms of a dead man.

He waited, counting off fifteen minutes by seconds in his mind. Sixteen minutes. Twenty. This was a big step. But it would change the life of Raymond Shamley.

He got out of bed, and walked through the quiet, dark corridor. He stopped before their door. Inside, distinctly, he could hear them making love. She was keeping him off guard.

He turned the well-oiled knob noiselessly and the door opened inward.

Then he snapped on the wall light.

"Get him, Ray! Kill him!" she said, leaping from the bed. She was naked, the nightgown twisted under the sheets, and her body gleamed faintly with perspiration. "Shoot him!"

Ernie moved quietly in the bed, and withdrew something from under his pillow. Ray watched quietly. It was a sheaf of bills. A thick sheaf.

"Did you make them small bills?" Shamley asked.

"Nothing larger than a fifty," Ernie said,

tossing the money to the foot of the bed. He turned over, and it might have been that he was asleep.

Recognition dawned on Betty's face with black horror. Her dark, lovely skin paled down several degrees. "What are you doing? You can't do this to *me*... I found you... I asked you to... no, you can have me, and all the money..."

Ray shook his head gently. "I'm sorry. Really. But how long do you think I could trust you. In a few days you'd decide you didn't need a broken-down musician, and then you'd say to hell with me.

"I wouldn't be able to do a thing. I couldn't talk, and I'd be out in the cold again. I want that band, Betty. I want it worse than anything. Even you."

"He'll double-cross you!" she screamed, her hands flat on her belly in terror. "He'll cross you and tell the police you stole the money."

"No, I made sure of that. I have a signed statement by your husband that he was the one who engineered this, and he has one from me that I executed it. That way I can't blackmail him... that way he can't turn me over to the police. It's a very satisfactory arrangement."

"But you can't... don't... you'll have nothing without me!"

"I'll always have my music," he said. He turned on the radio on the bureau, and the thick, heady sounds of New Orleans blues welled into the room. Ernie lay on his stomach, half-asleep, secure that he was safe, and free again of the conniving witch he had married.

"What good will it do..." she pleaded, starting toward him. "What good..."

He fired low, catching her in the thigh with the first shot. The second bullet caught her in the stomach and doubled her over. Her hands kneaded the soft flesh of her belly, and then the crimson was spilling out between her fingers. The third shot took her high in the chest, spinning her, throwing her against the wall.

She slid down the white wall, leaving an ugly, black-red smear that followed her to the floor.

Yet she was not dead. The cat still clung to life. Bayou Betty looked up, her eyes glazing, her life pumping out of her, and she managed to gasp:

"I...taught...you..."

It was incredulity, and he replied, turning to the money on the bed:

"You taught me real good."

The radio blared its sounds, and there was one instant of high riff, of deep blues, and that note was for the bayou cat.

Gang Girl

I'M BACK with Moms now, and I get sick to my stomach when I think of what I did. I only did it because I was lonely and because I loved Puff. If it hadn't been for him, well...

Things might have been different.

Moms doesn't say anything; she won't judge me. But a lot of them look at me when I go down the street, and I can hear their dirty whispers floating behind me.

All those wise guy, stuck-up big shots out there! *They* should try living where I live. Down where the cold off the river mixes with the stink of the fish, and you always have a rotten-fish odor in whatever you do.

After a while it gets in your hair, and your nose, and you taste it when you eat, and when you go to sleep you smell it all night! It gets so bad you want to run away from the neighborhood, just to breathe some fresh air.

Maybe that's what made me walk so much, the day I met Puff.

I hadn't had much to do with the kids in the street. Dad's been dead six years now. When I wasn't in school, I was taking care of the house or my baby sister, while Moms worked.

So when I walked out of my neighborhood, and wandered into Eagle turf, I didn't even know I'd gone over a line.

Was that only six months ago? It seems like six years!

I was just walking; I didn't know where I was

going, just so long's I was going away from that fish-stink! I must have walked farther away from my section than I'd ever gone before.

I passed a lot of boys on the streets. At first the remarks they kept makings got past me. I was thinking, and I was lonely, and I just wanted to walk.

I was going past a drug store, and there were two boys leaning against a window. I heard one of them say, "Man! Hand me some of *that* on a plate, and I'll eat it up with a big spoon!" Then the other fellow laughed and called me something dirty.

I'd never been around the streets too much, and I'd never heard anybody speak to girls that way. I started to walk past, but the one who'd called me a dirty name grabbed me by the arm.

"Let go!" I yelled.

"Come on, Tight-Jeans," he said and laughed, pulling me to him. "Whyn'cha come with old Toby and me in my car? We'll take ya out and buy ya a hamburger!"

"Get the hell away from me!" I screamed, scratching at his face. He had me tightly around both wrists, and I struggled, but couldn't pull loose. So I kneed him in the groin.

He let loose fast, then, and clutched himself. His buddy, the one he'd called Toby, grabbed me by my ponytail and gave me a stiff crack across the face. He hauled back to smash me some more, but I bit him.

He was howling, and they were both getting ready to belt me again, when three other boys came tumbling across the street. They were all wearing black leather jackets, with metal stars and studs on them. The word "Cavaliers" was written in white across the backs.

"It's Eagles!" howled one of the black-jacketed boys, a big kid with a blond crew-cut. He slammed across the street and hit the boy named Toby in the mouth with his fist. Toby sailed backward and went through the drug store window. The other kid still looked like the kick I'd given him hurt a lot, but it didn't stop the other two Cavaliers. They picked him up by arms and legs and heaved *him* through the window on top of Toby!

"Come on, let's get the hell outta here!" mumbled the boy with the blond crew-cut, grabbing me by the arm. Somehow, I trusted him more than the other two. I ran with them, turning down an alley between two apartment buildings, and hopping a fence.

After a while we stopped to catch our breath. The blond boy turned to me. "It's okay now. We're in Cavalier turf.

"You're new around here, aren't you?" he asked. He had a nice face. It was square and strong-looking; when he smiled his eyes crinkled at the corners.

"I'm not from around here," I answered, still not sure of them. I was puffing from all that running.

"What's your name?" he asked.

"What's yours?"

"I asked first," he replied, hooking his square hands into the back pockets of his jeans. He grinned.

"Julie," I answered. "Julie Grendon. Now what's yours?"

"They call me Puff. This is Flip, and the short one there is Weepy," he said, waving a hand at his friends. "We're members of the Cavaliers," he said, proudly. "What were you doing in Eagle territory?"

"What's Eagle territory?" I asked. He looked at me in surprise. I was real stupid in those days.

"For a chick as cool-looking as you, you're pretty square, ain'tcha?" he asked.

I drew myself up in anger. "So who asked ya to speak to me, wise guy? I was doing okay till you came along!" I started to leave, but he put a hand on my arm. He didn't try to hold me, just to stop me for a second.

I turned around and looked at him. I could tell right off that he was sorry. "I—I didn't mean that," he stammered.

"Oh, that's okay," I said. I knew he didn't want to look punk in front of his buddies. It had taken him a lot to apologize.

The little fellow, Weepy, sat down on a garbage can and asked, "Don't you know who the Eagles are?" The way he asked it, it sounded like they were someone real important.

"No," I answered. "Who are they?"

"They're a new gang that just got together. Bunch of real slobs. They been raiding our turf about three months now," said Flip. He clenched his fists as he spoke.

"One of these days we're gonna lean on those crumbs—real hard!" added Puff, his eyes getting harder. He looked nasty when he was mad. But I couldn't help liking him.

They nodded at one another, as though they'd agreed on something silently. "Come on, I'll buy ya a shake," said Puff, taking my hand. "Then I'll let ya in on the score around here. If you're going to be hanging around the Cavaliers, you better know what gives."

I hadn't really considered it, but being around the Cavaliers—and that meant being around Puff—seemed like a real cool idea.

"Sure. I'd like a shake," I said.

Over a milk shake they told me about the rival gangs, and how we were now in Cavalier turf, which bordered Eagle territory.

"What were you doing over in their neighborhood if you're not supposed to cross in there?" I asked them.

Weepy started chuckling. "Woman, we were on a *raid*! We was gonna bash a few skulls, that's why!"

These boys were different from the ones I'd known. All the kids I'd ever hung around with were just happy-go-lucky, always laughing at something silly. These kids were *so* different. They seemed mad at everybody, yet I knew they liked me, and wanted me for a friend. I liked that, too. I wanted to be in with a bunch of kids who all knew each other and had something in common.

I'd never belonged to a group of my own, and these kids seemed like lots of fun.

Flip leaned across the booth, twisting the

straw from his shake. "How'd you like to be a Cavvy Deb?" he asked.

Puff put his hand on Flip's chest and shoved him back. "I saw her first," he said, pointing his finger at Flip with meaning. "*I'll* ask her!"

"I don't know," I answered. "What is it?"

"We've got what you'd call girl's auxiliaries in the Cavaliers," explained Puff. "We call 'em the Debutantes, or just Debs for short. The Cavvy Debs, see?"

I smiled. "Sure, I understand. What do I have to do to join?"

Puff shrugged his shoulders, said, "Nothing. Just say you want to be a member. Then we take you over and introduce you to the other kids. Then you're a Cavalier—after initiation, of course—and you can come to all our dances, and on our rumbles, and like that."

It sounded terrific. "That sounds like fun," I told him. "I guess I'd like to join."

Puff told me I should come to the club rooms the next night, and I'd get introduced around. He told me where they were, and what I should wear. Then he offered to walk me home. I said okay.

On the way home, Puff said hi to a lot of kids, both girls and guys, and a lot of them weren't wearing Cavalier jackets. "How come?" I asked him.

"Simple," he said. "Sometimes the cops are looking for some of us, and it isn't smart to advertise. If they don't know we got a club, they can't pin anything on us."

"What—do they want to—pin—on—you?" I

asked slowly, nervously.

He waved his hand carelessly. "Oh, *you* know. Stuff."

"What kind of stuff?" I asked again.

Puff turned on me, real mad. "Look, Julie. You gotta mind your own business, not ask personal questions till you're in the club. *You* know!"

I was so surprised, I wanted to walk away, but he'd been so nice to me, I decided not to.

He left me off at my building, and said he'd see me the next night. He warned me to cut around Eagle turf. By this time I was smart enough to know what he meant.

Next day I was in an oppressive fog. I mean, it was Saturday, and I was supposed to clean the house. But I just couldn't stop thinking about Puff, and the Cavaliers, and the new things that had suddenly come into my life, I forgot everything else, I guess. Moms came back from shopping and I was still lying around, eating an apple and thinking about the night before.

Moms is pretty good about those things. "How come you didn't clean up like I asked you, Julie?" she said, putting down her packages.

"Moms," I said slowly, "do you know anything about the Eagles?" She looked at me with a puzzled expression for a minute, so I added, "You know, what they call the club! The Eagles club."

"They hang out in the streets, don't they, Julie?"

"I suppose so," I said. Moms had that look.

"You aren't hanging around with them boys, are you, Julie?" She looked worried. So I gave her the answer she wanted.

"No, Moms. I just heard some kids talking about them, and I was—well, *you* know—wondering like." I shrugged the whole thing off. But Moms wasn't put down that easily.

She came over, where I was lying on the couch, and she plopped down next to me. "Julie," she said, "I know things haven't been so hot, with Dad gone and you having to watch out for things while I work. I know you don't have much fun. And you're a good-looking girl—you *should* have more fun. But these are bad streets we live in, Julie. The kids are wild and they don't know no respect for their elders. You got to promise me you won't go near any of those roughnecks in the gangs."

"Sure, Moms," I said. I took her hand in mine, cause I knew she liked that. It made her think I was her little Julie-baby again.

Then she smiled down at me, and patted me on the rump. "I'll fix lunch," she said, getting up. She looked so tired; I couldn't bear it!

"I'll clean up now, Moms," I yelled to her as she went though the door to the kitchen.

A couple minutes later, Moms called in to me, while I was dusting the television set: "Where you going tonight, Julie dear? You going out?"

"Uh-huh," I answered.

"Where you planning on going?" she asked. I could tell she was still worried, so I answered, "Oh, there's a dance down at the Y. Thought I'd fall over there and see who's around."

She said oh that's nice, and went back to her cooking.

I hate lying to Moms like that—but she just doesn't understand!

When I showed up at the club rooms, Puff and the others were already there.

The club room was a big apartment at the back of a bowling alley. It must have been an apartment house once, and they'd cut it up when they put in the bowling alley, because I had to go around the back, through the passage between buildings, to get into the apartment. The place was real big and classy-looking. It was six rooms, all with high ceilings, and the kid had fixed it up so there was a living room like, and bedroom pads in case any of the kids had to sleep overnight. There was a kitchen, and a bar in the living room. The whole setup was the coolest!

The place was dim, with cigarette smoke, and I could see couples dancing close together in the dusk. I could also smell the sour-sweet odor of dope. *That* I didn't like!

Puff met me at the door and introduced me around. All the kids had nicknames like Cherry, Smooch, Clip, Frogo and even one girl they called Hike. After I'd met all the kids, Puff took me aside.

"I didn't think you was comin'," he said.

"I said I'd be here, and I'm here. I had to help Moms put the kid sister to bed, and wash the dishes." I liked him more this time than when I'd seen him before, and it didn't seem strange explaining what kept me.

"Still wanna be a Deb?" he asked. I could see he wanted me to say yes. I was going to anyhow.

I nodded my head, and he broke into that crinkly smile. Gee, he was cute! I'd known lots of boys in school, but none of them had been as sharp as Puff. He was a real smooth character.

Right then somebody put on a record, and the kids started dancing again. It was "fish," where you dance close and grind, and I didn't know whether I should do it with Puff, 'cause I'd only just met him.

But he didn't give me a chance to think. In a second he had me in his arms, up close, and we were dancing. He was as smooth a dancer as he was good-looking.

When the record was over, Puff asked me, "You want something to drink?"

I told him I didn't drink. He kind of laughed, said *everybody* either drank or was on pot. I knew what pot was—dope—but I didn't want any part of that jazz! So I told him I'd have a beer, if they had one.

He went into the kitchen and dug me out a can, and opened it for me. I thought he'd bring me a glass with it, but I guess they didn't have any, because he just brought back the can alone. I took it and thanked him. He was watching me, so I took a good healthy swallow.

I don't like beer—it's too sour—but everybody else was chugging the stuff, so I figured I would, too. After a while I sort of liked the taste of it, even though it made me feel prickly inside. My head felt funny, too.

———•———

In a few minutes a kid even bigger than Puff, named Chunk, turned off the record player and said the meeting was now gonna come to order.

Then everybody sat down on chairs or on the floor, and they started the meeting. It was run just like the girls club I used to belong to in school. There was a report of the last meeting, where they'd discussed terms of a war with another gang. Then they called for new business. One of the kids stood up and asked how funds for the dance were doing. Chunk—I guess he was the Prez—called on a thin, short kid with glasses to give a report.

He told everybody that the dance was going to be next Saturday night, and almost all the dough had been raised. They'd bought all kinds of stuff, and they were going to start decorating the club rooms Wednesday. Everybody cheered, and the kid sat down, grinning all over.

This was great! Just the kind of bunch I liked! I couldn't see why Moms had warned me away from the kid gangs. They were swell! They were always doing something, and they weren't afraid of anybody. When Puff put his arm around me, I didn't pull away.

Then this Chunk looked over at me and started grinning; right then I didn't care for him one bit. I felt cold and naked when he stared at me. "I guess the initiation is next," he announced.

Everybody looked at me. All the girls, most of

all. Puff pulled his arm tighter around me, and if I was scared for a minute there, I wasn't any more.

"Is there anyone who wants to become a member of the Cavvys or the Cavvy Debs?" he asked, looking straight at me.

I didn't say anything till Puff gave me a nudge and whispered, "You say, 'I do.'" So I said it.

In about a minute cold, they had a circle cleared out in the center of the room. All the lights but two went off. Those were dim ones, and I couldn't see too clearly through the smoke.

"You sure you wanna join, now?" I heard Chunk's voice from the front of the room. "To always be a member, and be true to the Cavaliers, and always to be square with everyone in the club?" I didn't know what else to say, so I told him, yes, that's right.

Then he said, "Strip to the waist!"

I stood up real quick, and said, "The hell with you! You think you're gonna get a free show, you're crazy!"

The next minute two of the boys had me by the arms and a couple girls unbuckled my belt and started slipping my sweater up over my shoulders. When they let go for a second, so they could slip the sweater over my arms, I kicked one of them. Before I could do any more, though, they had me again, this time they had the sweater off.

Then they unfastened my bra and I felt the cold of the room all over me. My skin started to prickle. I shut my eyes so I wouldn't see the way the boys were looking at me.

One of them whistled real low, but I heard Puff, with a real strained voice, tell him to shut his yap.

"We don't wanna hurt ya, Julie," said Chunk, and I opened my eyes a little bit. I couldn't see him very well through the smoke and stuff, but I heard him very clearly. "It's just that this is part of the initiation. All the girls gotta go through it. There's better parts comin'!"

Then he laughed, and so did all the others. I wondered what they meant. I wasn't going to let any slob like that think I was chickie, so I told to get whatever it was over with.

Then they let me go, faded back into the circle and I saw about seven girls coming into the cleared space, with their belts in their hands. They had 'em wound around their fists, and they were swinging them. I guess I must have screamed or something, 'cause in a minute they were on me, swingin' with all their might! They kept at it like they hated me for a good five minutes, till Chunk yelled, "Okay, okay! That's enough! Get away from her!"

But, oh! When they got through, I was lying on that dirty floor, with all those ciggy butts around me, bleeding like a skinned fish and cryin' like a bottle-baby.

I'd never seen anything like it. While they were doing me, the room had been jumping! The guys and drags had been coughin' it up something wild. Screaming and yelling and telling 'em to get me with the buckles. But when it was over, everybody was around, holding me up, wiping off my face, plugging up the cuts and bruises. And there wasn't a guy there tried to get a cheap feel while they were doing it.

I hated them, right then, 'cause they were mean and vicious; but when they all came around me, talking low and saying I'd been real wild and taken it like a cool chick, I felt better. My back felt like blazes, but I could stand it.

I got up and wiped my eyes with my hand. They moved away a little bit and I said, "Who the hell's got my bra?"

They handed it to me and I put it on. My sweater, too. "What now?" I said real sullen and looking at the floor.

"Now you gotta pick your stud," said Chunk.

"Whaddaya mean I gotta pick my stud? I'm not a slave or something! If I want a guy, I can get him on my own, and I don't need anything from you creeps!"

There was a lot of boo about that, and I heard one guy yell to toss me out on my can, but Chunk told him to shove it, that I'd been cool and they needed chicks like me.

I knew what the pitch was then. He wanted me. That Slob! I'd have rather died than be seen on the streets with him! I didn't give a you-know-what if he *was* the Prez of the Cavaliers!

"Okay, man," I said. "I'll pick." Then I walked over and put my arm though Puff's, holding it tight to my side. I was praying he didn't have a steady drag already.

He looked down at me and a big crinkly grin shot out all over his face. He was so smooth. "She's mine, man, and I *want*!" Puff said.

Chunk looked like somebody'd put a pin though his nose, but he waved a hand and said, "Okay, Puff, she's your woman. Take her in back."

That rocked me for a second. What was *this* now?

I was scared witless for a minute, but Puff whispered in my ear, "Come on, you don't have to be scared. I won't bother ya."

So I went with him. We walked out of the living room, with all those chicks and studs laughing and giggling. We walked into one of the bedrooms, and Puff locked the door behind us.

He sat down on the edge of the bed, looking at me as though he was a kindergarten kid or something. He looked like a real little kid, so help me! "You know what's supposed to be, don'tcha?" he asked.

I nodded, and he opened his hands as if to say, well, it's up to you.

I shook my head at him. "Uh-uh, Puff. I dig you—you know that—but nobody's laid it to me yet, and they ain't gonna till I've got a ring to make it right. You understand, don'tcha?"

Then he smiled, and I don't think I was ever so glad to see anybody smile at me like that.

"Play it any way you like, Julie," he said, and then he wasn't a Cavvy any more. He was just a sweet guy, and I'd almost do it for him. I went over and sat down next to him and he put his arm around me.

Next thing I knew, they were banging on the door, telling us we'd had enough time in there.

Puff got up and wiped my lipstick off his face with his hankie. "Man! Where'd you learn to neck like *that*?" he said, grinning big again.

"Oh, I been around," I answered, real wise. He kept smiling, and I stood up, smoothing out my skirt. I kissed him again, hard.

"You really want me for your drag?" I asked.

"Really, Julie," he said, real sincere.

"Okay," I replied, "but you better be on the level with me, 'cause that's the way I like it."

He grinned like a big clown and we went back into the living room. Everybody patted me on the back, and a few of the guys thought they were entitled to kiss me. I cooled *that* idea, real fast.

Best of all, they called me Julie, and everybody said I was welcome to the Cavvy Debs. I was in! I belonged! For the first time in my life!

I almost cried, so help me God!

Next six months were terrific. I went with Puff everywhere. Sometimes we'd go alone, and sometimes on Club drags, with all the gang.

Once in a while there'd be a rumble, and once I toted Puff's piece—his zip gun—back and forth to a war.

It was a big rumble with the Corkscrews, from over near the park, and the cops got wind before we even got in a few pots at the crumbs. So I had to shove Puff's piece into my garter belt, and kite outta there fast! No cop would search a chick, so I got away clean.

Puff got picked up, though, and they took him down to the station.

I sweated it out till they let him out. The day he was sprung, I waited, biting my nails, worried to death.

Then I heard him in the street. "Hey, Julie! I gotta record!" I ran over to the window and looked out. He was down there, grinning, yelling up at me. I stuck my head out and squealed with love.

"Puff! I'll be right down!"

I ran down, hardly touching the stairs, and kissed him right there in the street. I was so glad to see him! "How'd they treat you?" I asked.

He shrugged, looked like a real hero. "Oh, they kicked me around a bit. One of them lousy slugs tapped me with his nightstick, but it didn't bother me."

He pulled his T-shirt up and showed me the bruise on his ribs. I swore, and told him I'd fix it up.

"C'mon upstairs."

We walked up, arms around each other, and Puff whistling a real cool number. When we got to the apartment I shoved open the door and yelled to Moms, "Hey! Where's the Band-Aids and stuff?"

She came out of the kitchen, wiping her hands on a towel. "What's *he* doing here?" She asked, real bad.

"He's my man. I've got a right to have him—"

"You've got *no* rights at all!" she screamed, throwing the towel on the sofa. "I told you I didn't like them street hoods, that you'd get into trouble running with them, and here you bring one into my home!"

"Moms—" I started, but she cut me off.

"Moms, hell!" she snapped. It was the first time I'd ever heard my mother swear. "If you wanna ruin yourself, okay, you do it! But don't bring none of them dirty killers in here!"

I got sore then, and yelled something awful at her. Then Puff and I fell out, real fast. We stomped down the stairs, and I was madder'n I could be!

"C'mon, I'll take you to a show," Puff suggested.

"No, I don't wanna go to any show," I said. I was all ready to scream.

Things seemed to be going downhill so fast I couldn't stop them. I'd never fought with Moms. I'd never gotten her mad at me, or heard her swear like that. I'd never hung out in candy stores or pool rooms like I was doing now. I'd always been around the house in case Moms needed help—now I never was. I'd always had the people in our block smile at me, but now they just avoided me, didn't even say hello.

There was Puff, too. He wasn't like I'd thought kids in the Cavvys would be; none of them were. I was finding that out. They were smart-alecky and always looking for a fight—always wanting to start trouble. It wasn't fun and excitement as I'd thought it would be.

I was scared now.

I turned and looked at Puff. "I want to quit the Cavvys," I said real quietly.

Puff just looked at me for a second. He didn't say anything, but I knew what he was thinking:

nobody quits the club. "Maybe we better go talk to Chunk," Puff said, looking down at the sidewalk. He wouldn't look me in the eyes, and I knew he was scared, too. He didn't like bucking the gang. But he was a Cavalier, and he had to do what the gang wanted, even when it came to me.

"Can't you quit, too, Puff?" I felt like I was going to cry if something didn't happen soon.

"Yeah, if I'd like my brains spread out on the street," he answered, jerking his head with meaning. It was tough for guys who wanted out. It was tougher for girls.

"Okay," I told him, "let's go talk to Chunk."

We passed a couple of Cavaliers on the street, and Puff asked them if they'd seen Chunk. They told him Chunk was down in the pool room, shooting some snooker.

Puff took me to the club rooms, pushed me down in a big armchair and told me to wait. He said he'd be right back.

When he closed the door, I got more scared than I'd ever been before—even at the initiation. I started thinking about what I'd done.

I'd joined a kid gang—a gang of juvenile delinquents. I bit my lower lip when I put it into words, but I had to say it: "You're just a tramp," I told myself. "You run with killers and muggers and thieves!"

I thought, *I'll bet Dad would love that if he was alive, wouldn't he?* Then the picture of my Pop, real clear, and looking just like he looked before he died, came into my mind, and I started to cry.

"I didn't know, I didn't know!" I kept repeating, crying and beating at the arm of the chair with my fist.

I was still crying when Chunk came in. I didn't see him open the door, but suddenly I heard him say, "You stay out for a while, Puff." I looked up, and real fright must have been in my face, because he looked at me with tight lips and dark eyes. He locked the door.

I looked up and caught a quick reflection of myself in the mirror near the door. I wasn't pretty any more. My face was puffy and red and swollen from crying. My hair was a mess.

"I wanna hear you wanna punk out of the club," Chunk said, sitting down on the arm of the sofa.

I nodded my head. His face muscles tightened, one of them in his jaw jumped. He looked angry and his eyes were like black ice.

"Why ya wanna quit?" He seemed so damn smug!

I got mad then. Mad because I'd sworn at my mother; mad because I'd become something I hated; mad because I was lonely again. I'd come to them looking for friends, and I was merely something to neck with—*a piece of meat!*

"I want to quit because you're nothing but a bunch of bums and crooks! Because of you, Puff's got a record with the cops! That isn't fun! I didn't want that kind of fun! I thought you had dances and like that; I thought you were all friends. But you're not. You're always looking for someone to beat up, or some store to rob, or some girl you can make. You and your stupid rumbles—"

I was screaming at him, and the tears had started again. I guess I scared him more than anything, because he got off the sofa and grabbed me by both arms and started shaking me.

"Listen, you little broad! When you join the Cavaliers you *stay* in the Cavaliers till we say you can quit! How'd you like to live in the neighborhood without any protection from the gang? Huh? How'd ya like that? You'd be scared to go to the store for your old lady for fear someone'd jump ya!"

"I don't care, I don't care, I don't care!" I was screaming.

Then he slapped me to stop my noise. It hurt like the devil and it only made me cry more. That was when I heard Puff banging on the door.

"Lemme in, lemme in!" I heard him yell.

"In a sec!" Chunk yelled back. He pushed me into the chair and leaned over, talking real earnest.

"Julie, we *need* you in the club. We need all you Debs. To tote our pieces, to get dope to us about the rumbles. And if you stay in, Puff'll stay in. And we like you, too." He added the last almost as if it didn't matter.

That was when I'd realized they'd never let me quit. I was in the club to stay. And if I didn't do what I was told, well…

The scars from my initiation were still all over my back.

Then Chunk turned away and unlocked the door. Puff came charging in, saw me crying and turned on Chunk. "What the hell ya think you're doin'? I asked ya to say a few words to her, not to beat her up, you lousy—"

"Shut up, wise guy, I didn't beat her up. I just shook her a little to get some sense into her dumb head." Chunk was bigger than Puff, and I didn't want them to fight.

I'd started hiccupping, because I'd cried so much, but I mumbled, "It's true, Puff; he only slapped me to make me stop crying."

Puff backed off a little, still staring at Chunk in anger. "Come on," He said, not looking at me, still staring at Chunk with fire in his eyes. "We're getting out of here."

Out on the street, we walked for a little while in silence.

Then Puff turned to me, stopping me, and said, "Look, Julie, you know why the club won't let you quit. You're a girl, and well, you know what they want girls for." He seemed embarrassed, so I gave him a thin smile. "To most of those guys, girls are only worth what they can get from them. But you mean more than that to me, Julie. Honest to God! Don't quit the club, Julie, please!"

I knew what he meant. I leaned across and gave him a kiss on the cheek.

He smiled the crinkly smile and picked me up, swinging me around in circles till my skirt went up around my legs. "Julie, Julie, Julie," he said, real fast, swinging me, "I love you, Julie!"

I didn't even know we were in the middle of the sidewalk. I just hugged him so close I thought my ribs would bust.

"I love you too, Puff!" I cried.

He set me down, and looked into my eyes. There was so much happiness in his face, I wanted to start crying all over again. Because no one had ever made him happy before, and I guess the same for me. Right then, I'd have given him my life if he'd asked for it.

"There's a Cavvy dance at the Y tonight!" he said, snapping his fingers. "I forgot all about it! It's to celebrate all the kids gettin' out of the pokey. Wanna go?"

The thoughts about how the Cavaliers were always starting fights and hurting people, came to me again. I didn't want to get back in with them as strong as I'd been.

But there was the feeling of belonging to the group, of being one of the crowd. I didn't want to be left out. And Puff seemed to want me to go so badly, wanted to show how much he loved me, that I couldn't make up my mind.

I looked at Puff. He could tell I was having a hard time deciding.

"Please," he asked, real softly.

I loved him so much. He was my guy, and I wanted to go everywhere with him, show him I could belong to the Cavvys if he could.

I suddenly felt light and gay and wanted to dance on top of the clouds. I grinned. "Sure!"

We started off down the street, Puff whistling that cool number again, but as we passed Puff's building, he asked me to wait a minute. If I'd known what he was going after, I'd have never waited a second! "I'll be right back," he said, "gotta pick somethin' up."

I sat on the steps; in a minute I found myself whistling the same tune as Puff. It was the first time in my life I didn't have to watch out for my kid sister, or have responsibilities I didn't want. I knew I could rely on Puff's strength. He was a wonderful guy! And if some of the Cavvys weren't the best, well, there were enough kids in the club to like!

Then Puff came bounding down the stairs, out into the street. He jumped over my head as he went across the front stoop! I saw him shoving something into his pocket, but I didn't know what it was.

"Let's go, baby doll," he said happily, and we started off again.

We linked arms and I heard him say, "What a ball *this* is gonna be tonight! Whatta ball!"

It was pretty dim at the Y. They don't know how to decorate the gym so it's intimate-like, without being pitch-black; but it was nice anyhow. They had a lot of good records, and everything was going just fine, till the Eagles made it on the scene.

I was dancing with Puff, up close and really in love with him. When the number finished, Puff said, "I'll be right back, honey," and he walked away toward the shower rooms. I moved over to the wall and started talking to a couple of other Cavvy Debs. We were waiting for our drags to come after us, when I spotted one of the boys that had bothered me in front of the drug store that day I'd first met Puff.

"Hey!" I said, jabbing one of the girls in the ribs. "Those are Eagles! What're they doing here tonight?"

"Oh, man!" answered the girl—it was Hike—almost rubbing her hands together. "What a blast this's gonna be! The boys'll kill 'em!"

Right then another record started, and like he was magnetized to me, that kid turned, looked right in my face. I felt my heart stop as he walked over, but I couldn't say anything. There were three of them together.

"How's about a dance?" he asked, leaning in close to me. I could smell garlic all over him and I wanted to be sick, but before I could even say no, he'd whirled me out on the floor, was dancing real tight.

The other two Eagles had grabbed the Debs I'd been standing with.

"Lemme go!" I snarled in his ear. He laughed real low, and I hated that slob worse than anyone I'd ever known. "Lemme go! My drag'll be here in a minute and he'll do what he did to you before."

He pushed me away a little bit and looked at me carefully. "Well," he grinned, "if it ain't the little chick that got me put through a window! Where's this big hero of yours?"

I couldn't say anything. But out of the corner of my eye I could see a whole bunch of Cavvys, standing together near the wall, talking and pointing my way.

A second later Puff pushed off and came over fast.

"Get the hell away from her!" he growled, grabbing the Eagle by his shoulder and flinging him away. The kid fell to one knee.

The Eagle slid back, on one knee, reached into his jacket pocket and came up with something thin and long. "You're gonna get slit like a peapod!" he said, real dirty. Then he raised his hand real slow, so we could watch the knife come up, and pressed the button. The knife went *snick!* and sprang open, the colored lights in the ceiling glinting off it.

Puff stepped back fast. The Eagle started to rise, crouching. Then Puff let his arm slide loose in his sleeve, and *his* knife slipped into his hand. The switch clicked open, and I felt like screaming. There was going to be a horrible rumble. And over me!

I didn't want this! It was like a nightmare. A minute before everything had been okay, now there was gonna be blood all over everything. I was terribly afraid it would be Puff's blood.

"No!" I squeaked.

"Out!" snapped Puff, motioning me back.

I stepped back, and they circled. Few people had noticed what was coming off, because it was pretty dim.

Then, just when I thought they were going to go at it, the Eagle straightened, said, "Not here. Out in the parking lot. Just you and me. A stand!"

Puff straightened up, too, and nodded his head. He looked harder than I'd ever seen him, and it frightened me a little. The Eagle went out, and I saw a whole bunch of his buddies follow him. They went outside fast, like someone had pulled their strings.

Then the Cavvys were around us, and Chunk was saying, "Okay. If it's a stand he wants, you stand with him, Puff. They make a move, we'll cream 'em good! There's twice as many of us as them! Come on!"

We started moving toward the door, all the Cavvys and their Debs. That gym cleared out real fast.

As we were moving out, Puff drew me aside and reached into his jacket pocket. He took out his zip. "I heard a tip they'd be here tonight," he said, "that's why I bagged this; hang onto it, Julie. If they pull somethin', use it. You're the only one I can really trust!"

I couldn't understand that. I thought Puff was a real Cavalier, and they were all his buddies. But he didn't seem to think he could depend on them in a tight place. I was all confused.

I took the home-made weapon, looked at it real quick before I shoved it into my sweater. I knew how to fire it, of course. Puff had showed me a couple times. It was a sawed-off car radio antenna on a block of wood, with a .22 bullet in it. It was easy to shoot, but I was scared.

"Puff..." I started, "let's get outta here! He might..."

He shook his blond head. "Uh-uh. This is for my honor, honey! I won't get hurt, don't worry. There's more of us than of them. Don't worry."

We went outside, into the parking lot, and made a big circle. The place was all lit up from the big spots that bordered the lot.

Puff and the Eagle were in the center of the circle, both of them with switches out. As I watched, unable to breathe, they began circling each other again.

"We play this man-on-man," yelled Chunk to the Eagles. They yelled back that was right, then started yelling for their boy—Budge—to carve Puff up! I slid the zip out of my sweater, held it close to me, and watched. I hardly felt the thing hurting me as I pressed it close. I couldn't take my eyes off him. I loved Puff, I really did, and I was scared white he'd be killed.

They circled a couple of times, tossing their knives from hand to hand, to confuse each other. Then the Eagle took two quick steps forward and slashed out with the switch. He came in low and ripped upward!

It whistled past Puff's neck, but he'd jumped back. Then they were in close, holding off each other's knife-hand. It was horrible! I was sorry we ever came to that dance, sorry I'd ever let Puff out of my sight (sorry for a second that I'd ever *joined* the Cavaliers)!

Then they broke and Puff charged Budge. He came in real low, slashing up with the switch, as Budge had done. But he was faster than the Eagle: it caught Budge on his upper arm, ripping through his shirt and jacket.

Blood started dripping out, and I felt my eyes begin to water, my mouth go dry. I knew I was going to vomit!

They weren't human beings—they were little killers!

Suddenly I heard a shout, and looked over behind a line of parked cars. About thirty guys and girls were pouring out from where they'd been hidden.

"Eagles! Eagles!" somebody shrieked, and the next thing I knew everybody had knives and zips and bottles; one kid had a raw potato all studded with razor blades, and they were all going at one another. The parking lot was filled with screams and the blast of zip guns.

It had been an ambush! The slobs, the dirty rats!

I pulled my eyes back to Puff and the Eagle. Puff had been startled by it all, and had taken his eyes off Budge. I turned just as Budge moved in on Puff, raised the knife, and drove it into Puff's back!

"*Puff!*" I screamed, as he fell over on his side.

I looked down at Puff. His face had the strangest expression I've ever seen.

He looked as though he'd been spanked, and didn't know why. He looked as though someone had stopped his doing something innocent. He looked bewildered. I don't know what he looked like exactly. There was only one thing I really knew, and everything else faded out as I realized it.

Puff was dead.

I didn't have time to think about it anymore, though. The next minute I heard sirens, and police headlights turned into the lot. Then cops were all over the place.

Somebody yelled, "Break! Leech out! It's the cops!"

Then a cop moved on the kid that had yelled, and he didn't get a chance to use his knife. One of the cops smashed him in the head with his nightstick as the boy raised the switchblade. The kid went down, his arms out in front of him like he was reaching for something.

I started toward Puff, not even knowing what I was doing, but a cop grabbed me around the waist, lifted me off the ground, yanked the zip out of my hand.

I thought of when Puff had lifted me up, and started crying worse than I'd ever done before. I couldn't stop the pain in my heart. He was dead, dead, dead!

Then I realized it was a cop, not Puff, that held me in the air. I started kicking and screaming. "Lemme go! Puff, Puff!" I screamed, but he carried me, kicking, to the police wagon and threw me in with the other kids. I was really too numb to know what had happened.

All I could see was Puff lying there.

Then I went through a line-up, and had my fingerprints taken, and what they call a mug shot, and finally Moms showed up at the station.

When they came to get me I was sitting there staring at nothing. I hadn't said a word to anyone in the cell block. They brought me into the waiting room, and Moms stood up, her face all white like someone had drained all her blood away.

I wanted to die, right then, for making her suffer so much. I ran to her, and buried my face against her coat, crying like I'd just been beaten. I felt so terrible.

"Oh, Moms, Moms!" I cried.

Then I felt her hand on my hair, and I knew everything would work out in time.

I'd fallen in with a bad crowd; run with killers, done things I'd be ashamed of all the rest of my life. I'd seen Puff killed, and that had been the worst of all.

There can't be anything right with gangs that kill nice guys like him. Right then I felt sorry for every kid in every gang, all over the country, and prayed in my mind they would find out how evil they were. As I'd found out. I only hoped they wouldn't have to find out the same way I had.

It was all a black nightmare, and I thought I'd cry for the next hundred years. But I felt Moms holding me, telling me everything was all right and that it was all over now.

And somehow, I knew she was right.

The Girl with the Horizontal Mind

(as by "Price Curtis")

AS FAR AS HER THIGHS WENT... so did I.

I would have gone further, but the window shade was partially pulled, and as I swung over onto her ledge, all I could see were those luscious legs.

Now hear me good: I'm not a lecher by any means. I mean, when you're twenty-one and healthy, and on summer vacation in the big city, you try to have a good time. That's all, just a good time. But this chick was something else again. I could tell, just from the slim taper of her legs, and the full, round whitness of her thighs. She was young, and I was young, and if it was possible for a college boy working as a window washer to put the make on such a choice item, I was the boy and she was the item.

The window was open.

I pulled at the window shade, and it rolled up with a *swish!* and flapped at the top of its roll.

I was staring into two of the most beautifully-tipped breasts the world has ever known. They were full and round and using the standard measure, three and a half milliboobs per handful. She was powdering them with a big pink puff, and as the shade snapped free she paused in mid-puff.

I grinned stupidly; what else could I do?

"Just what the bloody hell do you think *you're*

doing?" She snapped at him, not trying to cover herself. There was a lot to cover. She was well-laid-out.

"Window washer, miss. Sorry about the shade." I kept grinning at her, flexing what few muscles I had inside my T-shirt. I indicated my hooking set-up, my bucket, and my squeegee. "See?" I said again, "Window washer."

She glared at me a moment, and then growled, "Well, don't stand there *staring*, you clown. Go away!"

I shrugged, and moved on down the ledge to the next window. Wouldn't you know it. Her bedroom. She came in from the living room—intent on slipping into her bath robe or something—and there I was. Big as life. All of me.

There was something about her, something really definite in the tilt of her head, in the auburn shine of her pageboy hair, in the clear blueness of her eyes, something there that just said: *I wish I was lying down.*

Just as Goya's nudes would look ludicrous standing up, just as Botticelli's nudes would have looked foolish on their feet, this chick was made for the horizontal, and though she was a knockout standing upright, I knew that on her back she would make radiators boil over.

"You again?"

I grinned at her sheepishly, and made a futile flipping motion with my free hand. "Sorry," I said, "didn't realize you were coming in here."

"When I said go away, fella, I meant *away*! Not down the line to gawk some more."

"I can't help it," I said, in my best smooth-soap line. "Fate keeps throwing us together."

"And I'm going to throw you off that ledge if you don't stop peering at me." But she didn't move to cover herself, and she didn't move to get dressed. She had a very odd sparkle in those blue eyes, and I thought I recognized it.

That horizontal look.

"My name's Walt," I said conversationally. "Walt Tucker. I'm only a window washer on vacation. I go to school at—"

"Mister, I don't care if you're Enrico Fermi and you've just invented the A-bomb! Get the hell off my window before I call a cop!" But her hands went to her stomach, and pressed inward there, the fingers all but barely pressing around her navel. It was the sexiest goddam pose I've ever seen.

I unhooked and slipped a leg over the window ledge.

"Where do you think *you're* going?" she demanded irately...moving back to give me room to swing in.

"Well," I said, fiendish thoughts of that down-soft belly and those long legs rumbling in me, "since we seem to be such close acquaintances, I thought I might come in for a cup of coffee."

"Mister, I'm giving you just thirty seconds to get out of here, before I—"

But her eyes were sparkling, and Walt Tucker—alias The Tiger—never mistakes a look. I knew it was hare-brained, and the chick would probably screech rape as soon as I touched her, but it was a gamble. I reached out and took her by the arm.

She came into me as though we were magnetized. I got my mouth down on her full lips, and began nibbling the lower one. I've got a thing for lower lips. The chick can be a dog, as long as that lower lip is a full, soft one. This lip was the greatest, and this chick was a dream, anyhow.

She plastered herself against me, from mouth to thigh, and what there was of her was choice indeed. I felt the quivering of her belly even though my clothes, and her breasts pressed against my T-shirt impatiently.

I felt her arms go up around me, under my armpits, and she hooked her hands at my shoulders, thrusting her lower body against mine.

I suddenly realized we were standing in front of the open window. Not only could we be seen in sharp relief against the white apartment walls by everyone in the apartments surrounding, but I also had a co-worker, a schnook named Charlie, who might come looking for me any moment.

I disengaged our mouths, and she let loose a low, animal moan that set my hair to climbing. I'd been right, of course. She was just the type that digs, and what I'd thought was foolish prematurity in my coming inside, had turned out to be perception. She was a chick who thought horizontally.

She was trying to drag me backward, to the sofa, but I pulled back, setting her away from me for a moment. Wait a minute.

"Uh, hey, how about if I pull down the blind?" I said, moving toward it automatically, expecting no great objections.

"*Leave it alone!*" she screamed, and got between me and it faster than anything I've ever seen. "If you want to stay with me, leave it up!"

"But the whole damned neighborhood can see us!" I said, more than mildly baffled.

"Leave it … or get out!"

I looked at the window, and thoughts of Charlie, or the neighbors phoning the vice squad, of passersby in helicopters, came to me with frightening clarity. But her hips kept intruding on the view, and her breasts were coral-tipped and winking at me, so I shrugged.

To hell with it.

"C'mere," I said huskily. My throat had very suddenly gone dry.

She came to me, then, and all that coolness she had exhibited at first had turned to flame and smoke. All the mordant smartmouth that had been in her was turned into a quick, darting tongue that opened my mouth and sent lancets of fire coursing down through me.

I got a hand under her thighs, and lifted her in my arms. I'm six feet one, but she was a big girl, and I guess I staggered more than carried her. It wasn't very romantic, but I started to drop her gently onto the sofa, and she kept her arms around my neck.

I went down, right on top of her.

It was wondrously awkward at first, but I eventually joined her in her happy natural state. Her legs moved under me. Then there was great warmth and moistness, and she had her hands locked behind my back, the sharp, flaming nails ripping at me.

The moaning was continuous now, and just as the world shuddered itself into silence, she whispered in a hot, pulsing voice:

"My name is Julie…my name is Julie…love me, my name is Julie…"

At least it was nice to know who she was.

Her full name was Julie Ryan, which was as Irish as her auburn hair and flashing blue eyes. She worked as a governess for a pair of hideous little beasties in a palatial mansion uptown, and she got to her own apartment only on Wednesdays and Sundays.

For the record, I was tied up every Wednesday and Sunday. By Julie Ryan. Tied up by her long legs and full lower lip.

But there was something odd about her. Isn't there always? What it was with her, I couldn't quite name, but she never made love in the dark, and in fact she made love with the blinds up…and once with the cleaning woman in the next room.

It got to be pretty harassing.

But she was such a cool sketch, and she knew how to use that wicked body of hers so well, I didn't really give a damn.

I got used to it. Up to a point. Except…

One Sunday evening, we were lying there sharing a cigarette, the sheets hanging off the side of the bed, and she said, "Walt, do you want to make me happy?"

Now there'd been no mention of marriage, and I had thought we both understood that wasn't going to enter into this, but she said it so damned sincerely, I turned to her—she was still flushed from our bout—and answered, "Sure, honey, but I'm still in college; I've got hardly enough money for my—"

"Oh, you clown!" she said, and kicked at me with her free leg. "I'm not talking about that."

"Well, sure, I want to make you happy," I covered quickly. "I thought I was doing a pretty good job." I pinched her breast, and she squeaked in outrage.

"Then will you do something for me?"

"Depends."

"On what?" She drew in air and her breasts grew tighter, larger. My mouth constantly went dry around that chick.

"On what you want."

She got to her knees then. Have I mentioned she was a natural auburn type. Seems foolish to add it; she was the kind that wasn't much for duplicity.

"Come on," she said, taking me by the hand. I felt like getting out of the sack right then, about as much as I felt like playing Russian roulette with a fully loaded .32 Police Special.

"Aw, Julie," I carped, trying to haul her back into bed.

"No, come on," she said, and dragged me to the window. It was an early Sunday evening, and the street was filled with people either coming or going, but either way, people who would certainly have noticed two naked people.

Julie climbed out onto the wide ledge under her window. "Where the blazes are you going?" I asked.

"Come on, chicken," she coaxed me.

"The hell!" I said. "Not on your life."

"You want to see me again?"

Let's face it. I'm a coward. I had two more months in the city before I went back to college, and this set-up with Julie was just what the psychiatrist had ordered. I climbed out onto the ledge. She wasn't kidding.

I made love to her right there, in full view of anyone who happened to look up...in full view of everyone in the apartments above, below, around and behind. She kicked, moaned and arched her back in passion, and bit my shoulders and raked my back with her nails, and I thought sure as the devil we'd be arrested.

But we weren't, and oddly enough, it was the most satisfying, nerve-tingling session I've ever had.

When it was over, and the sweaty imprint of our bodies was all that was left on the ledge, she turned to me—inside—and asked: "Wasn't that good?"

What could I say. Yeah, it was good.

I'd been scared witless throughout.

In the next few weeks, I had Julie under bushes in the park, with a cop walking his beat nearby. On the roof of a small shed behind the Second Baptist Church, with a social going on inside the building proper. In a canoe on the lake. On the stairs of her apartment building at midnight. (So all right, it was midnight, but there was still a chance of someone discovering us!)

I got down to about 120 pounds and I had suddenly developed a tic in my right cheek. When window washing, I thought I'd fall a dozen times. I was becoming a nervous wreck.

Finally, after a fantastic night in an open-topped convertible (her employer's) in a drive-in movie, with her gorgeous nylon-clad legs hanging over the side of the car—during Mr. Magoo—I knew it had to be all over between Irish Julie Ryan and me. I couldn't stand the killing pace.

So I told her goodbye. It broke my heart, and my mind cried *Traitor!*—but she didn't seem to mind. In fact, Julie told me, as I stood by the door that night, "Walt, you're a chicken."

"Guess what," I replied, "you're right."

Then I left her.

She was gorgeous, and she was the best, pardon the expression, lay I ever had, but Julie Ryan had a serious fault: she couldn't make love well unless there was an element of extreme danger involved. She had to be afraid someone was going to discover her at it. Perhaps it was a throwback to her childhood when she'd made love to boys under the stairs in her home, and was afraid her folks would find her, but whatever it was, she had to have it rough, or it was no go.

I didn't really mind so much all the weird and dangerous places I made her, at first. I mean, being a window washer isn't the safest job in the world, so you can tell I'm not a complete fraidy-cat.

But what she had in mind was going too far.

I mean, you'd bolt *too*, wouldn't you, if a girl started talking dreamily about the Brooklyn Bridge and Macy's window?

An Episode of Sunbathers

RUMOR HAD IT THAT HE HAD LEFT the Santa Monica Sunbathers under force. There was nothing definite about it, and he certainly didn't *look* like that type, but what they said about Purvis Gregory was slanderous. He was sort of a medium type fellow. Medium colored brown eyes, and pimples on his back, and height that was just…well, ordinary height. His hair was thinning at the top, and he had a nervous habit of drawing down his upper lip tight over his teeth, when he talked and when he thought. So it didn't seem at all likely. But then, what was?

The rumors preceded Purvis Gregory's arrival at Health Hope Camp, and after the special meeting called to decide on his eligibility for entrance…the rumors followed him in a soft-blue cloud. The tests were conducted in private, as usual, but one of the girls who had been selected—Delores Marsche—spread the word through the camp later that day that the tiny bell hadn't even jingled once. So Purvis Gregory had been passed into Health Hope.

For bad or worse.

Nadine Tubell met him that afternoon, near the handball court. Nadine was a tall, slim Diana of a woman, whose breasts were sloping outcroppings most people called small, but which were, in actuality, more naturally upthrust than most women's in brassieres. Her

hair was long and, though brown, had been sun-
bleached till it shone with streaks of gold. Her
most attractive features were her slim thighs,
and full, rich calves. Her legs were delicious.

Nadine stopped in mid-slam, and turned
half-around to get a better view of Purvis
stumping toward the pool. He resembled a
chicken, hoppingly looking for a bit of corn. He
walked with arms locked behind his back, and
his head downcast.

*This is the big make-artist from the Santa
Monica crowd?* Nadine mused, not even slightly
impressed by the skimpy look of him; Purvis
was skimpy all over.

It should be pointed out that those carefree
residents of sunbathing camps, or "nudists," are
not of a lascivious turn of mind. The unclothed
body is to them a sign of health, not of sex.
There is as much normal sexual endeavor in
a colony of sunbathers, as anywhere else. But
promiscuity is frowned upon, as well as flagrant
display of erotic attitudes. This holds true for
the great bulk of sunbathers. Unfortunately,
it did not hold true for Nadine. And Nadine's
curiosity was aroused.

She slapped the handball at the wall in a sharp
reverse English motion, so that her companion
had to retrieve it from the bushes bordering the
court. "I think I've had it, Patsy," Nadine called,
low-hurdling the bushes, and striking out in
Purvis's direction. "Maybe tomorrow."

Nadine followed Purvis at a distance for a few
minutes, finally catching up to him as he passed
through a thick stand of bushes that separated

one length of path from another. She tramped up behind him, and laid her hand on the small of his back; as expected, Purvis leaped to attention in all quarters. He turned, and stared at her nonplussed.

"My name is Nadine Tubell. I'll bet you're Purvis Gregory, the new member, right? Well, hello, and welcome to Health Hope and I'm just trying to be friendly so why don't we go down by the edge of the forest and talk a while, hmmm?"

This exposition, delivered in one unbroken, continuous line of colored phrase and minute inflection, left Purvis even more shy and skittish than before.

But Nadine took his slim-fingered hand and led him off the path, down the hill, to the edge of the fine dark forest which surrounded the resort.

There she employed her philosophy of life: that it was not necessary—indeed, it was foolhardy—to employ clothing to make the female form enticing.

She sat Purvis down with his back to a birch tree—and began talking to him.

She began by turning her profile to Purvis Gregory. It was a charming profile, just bursting with ripples and tips and mounds and indentations. But somehow, Purvis Gregory was a stone statue. He fidgeted with his hands, looked at the chewed nails, plucked at a tiny scab on his knee. Nadine wondered if she'd suddenly sprung a bad case of loathsomeness.

She tried other tricks. Ancient tricks.

"Uh, excuse me, Miss Tubell," Purvis

stammered, suddenly leaping to his feet. Nadine sprawled, as she had wanted to sprawl, into the leaves. Unfortunately, she was alone.

"Well! I've *never*..." she began.

But Purvis Gregory was streaking down the path, toward the swimming pool, a fine jet stream of "Excuse me, excuse me, excuse me..." trickling after him in soft pastel hues.

Then the leaves stopped whirling, the branches settled back into place, the cold began to sweep through Nadine's pert bottom, and she knew. She was alone.

She got to her feet, feeling for the spot she knew would be black and blue tomorrow, and circumnavigated the current problem of Purvis Gregory. There was something but *definitely* wrong with that man.

She walked back toward the club house. It was getting chilly. It was on days of just this sort that she often had the completely lewd, out-of-place notion to...to...wear something!

Purvis Gregory was a mystery. He had turned down the warmest number on the lot, and seemed not at all inclined to partake of the other joyful treasures around him. It didn't seem that there was a lack of ability—hadn't all that gossip about the Santa Monica Sunbathers labeled him a rip and a rake? Hadn't Nadine said he had risen to her advances? Sure it did, and sure she did—but he was keeping his distance. It seemed almost purposeful.

Incident: Connie Winslow—the girl they called "Bubbles"—discovered Purvis flicking stones into the duck pond, and jumped him from behind. She reported he knew how to French kiss, that there was tremendous strength in his legs, that his chest was *not* hairless, merely blond, and that he had gotten away. She had received minor scratches and bruises from the twigs and pebbles, but Purvis was still inviolate.

Incident: Laurane Beamish met him behind the gymnasium (she suspected he was hiding) and managed to get him to take her in his arms. She reported no flutterings on his part, but she was certain a tiny squeal of pleasure escaped him. But when she had pulled him toward her, slipping down onto the soft green turf, he had leveled out for the woods again. Twenty-five minutes searching had not revealed his hiding place.

At the end of Purvis Gregory's third week at Health Hope, there was a definite crisis at hand. He was being hounded to shreds—his weight dropped off till it seemed he might pop into a non-existent state—and the women of the camp had but one mind. To score with Gregory.

It was obvious something would have to be done quickly.

Nadine did not speak to Purvis. She made certain no matter where he went, she was there. If he went to the pool, she was lounging at its side, stretching languidly, rubbing her body with suntan oil, till her skin was a luscious hue. If he went for a walk in the woods, she was sitting on a fallen log, combing her almost-blond hair, her smooth arms rising and falling in beckoning movements. Yet she did not speak to him, and became the only woman on the grounds who did *not* chase Purvis Gregory.

After a few days, it was apparent the scheme was getting to him. Gregory would stop short as he passed, and purse his lips. Several times he took a step toward her, as though about to speak, but then he would shake his head with infinite sadness and resolution, and walk on once more.

At the dances, when "rotation" was in effect, Nadine would make certain she dropped out, just as Purvis's turn came to dance with her. When he had passed down the line, she stepped back into the dance. This did not escape Purvis's notice. He fretted, his brow furrowed, he scratched himself more forcefully.

Finally, as it was destined, the situation came to a head. Purvis seemingly did not want to be made, but also seemingly did not want to be made an enemy. He was at heart a soft-shelled soul, whose greatest fear was that he was being stared at with displeasure. Had he been one of those unicellular paramecia swimming about here and there, he would have done nip-ups and handstands to please the watching amoebas. But he was a man—so it seemed!—and he took the most direct method for that species.

He approached Nadine one day.

She made certain the moment came when they were alone…in the gymnasium. Where tumbling mats were handy.

"Uh, excuse me, Miss Tubell," Purvis stammered, hands clasped behind his swayed back, "I've been meaning to speak to you about something."

Nadine turned what was intended as a cool eye on Purvis. Purvis was too troubled to notice the cool was a smolder.

"Ye-es?" she inquired haughtily.

"Well," he began slowly, finding his eyes inexorably drawn from her own to the protruding, heaving tips of her breasts, "I certainly hope that little—er—escapade we had in the woods a while back didn't anger you. I'm, I'm terribly sorry, but well…"

He fumbled into silence, shrugged his shoulders.

"I just hope you aren't mad at me," he concluded. "I don't think I'd like that."

Nadine brightened. "*Why* wouldn't you like that, Purvis? You don't mind if I call you Purvis, do you, Purvis?"

He acknowledged his not minding her Purvising. "Well… I just wouldn't, that's all."

Nadine moved slightly closer to Purvis Gregory, her eyes searching, her hands folded demurely across her bare belly. "Purvis, should I hold a grudge?" Her voice was pleasantly querulous. "There's no reason in the world… that is, if you *really* wouldn't like it…" She let the sentence dangle there fascinatingly.

Purvis, sensing the tenor of the discussion had changed, stammered and stumbled, and Nadine sensed his mood of recalcitrance was returning in full garb. She suddenly bolted away from him, bolted across the length of the gymnasium, and abruptly bolted the heavy gym doors. She stood arched with her back to the door, panting raggedly, and murmured, "Oh, brother...now...I...gotcha!"

Then the chase began.

And it must be said, in all fairness, that Nadine was the more elegant-appearing sprinter of the two. Around and around the big gymnasium they went, with Nadine so close behind Purvis, he was not able to open the doors in time.

Finally, as they rounded their twelfth turn, near the wrestling mats, Nadine gave a tremendous surge of speed, lifted herself into the air in a flying tackle, and crashed into Purvis Gregory's back.

The impact carried Purvis sidewise and forward, and in a moment they had landed, she atop him, on a pile of heavy wrestling mats. It must be admitted that Purvis did not move for a few moments, even though the heat of Nadine's body was moving. For Nadine was moving.

"Oh, I didn't want to, I didn't want to," Purvis moaned softly, his face against the wrestling mat. "This'll just start it all over again...but to *hell* with everything!"

With a joyous little cry of unrestrained animal fury, Purvis Gregory flipped and Nadine found, to her satisfaction, that it was true: Purvis Gregory was the *most*!

Naturally, being Nadine, she kissed...and told. In a few hours, after she had regained her equilibrium, she made paces to the girls, and told them.

She went on at great length, but long before she had lost her last listener, the hardier, more experimental ones, had gone in search of Purvis.

And his reserves must have been broken down from his contact with Nadine, and they must have found him...

...because of the twelve that went in search, twelve came back—much, much later—their faces glowing.

And by the end of the week, a problem had arisen: no woman in Health Hope would sleep with any other man but Purvis Gregory. Some men have talent for sculpture, some for trawling, some for baking...Purvis Gregory's talent was the most powerful single force for home-breaking the world had ever known.

The men at Health Hope were getting but *nothing*, and they naturally decided to get rid of Purvis Gregory. But before they could act they met an army of women at the gates of Health Hope.

"Who're you?" the men asked.

The women at the gate replied, "We're from the Santa Monica Sunbathers!" and one screamed, "Is he here?"

And in a short time, the story came out. The story of why Purvis Gregory had left the Santa Monica crowd. (It had not been the women who had thrown him out, and it had not been the men. Both had been unable to touch him.) It had been Purvis himself, who had wandered away. The men had been so incensed at his stealing their wives, *they* were ready to kill him—but fearing their wives' wrath, began beating *each other* up—and the women—who could only get at him after another woman had been there, and so had to wait in line—had taken to fighting for positions. (So he had left.)

The Santa Monica women had left their lovers and husbands, and followed Purvis here. And they were bound to follow him. Wherever he went. Because there was nothing else like him under the sun. He was the Pied Piper of Love.

And when, that night, the men of Health Hope—having bunked down the women of Santa Monica, and sent their own wives to bed with the strictest orders to stay there—went to fetch Purvis Gregory, to throw him out...they found him gone.

A sad and pathetic note was left for them to marvel at:

I'M SORRY THIS HAPPENED. IT ISN'T MY FAULT. THIS THING I'VE GOT IS TOO BIG! AND I'M AFRAID THIS IS JUST THE BEGINNING. AGAIN I'M SORRY.

PURVIS GREGORY

At first, the men laughed and cheered, clapped each other's naked backs, proclaimed a national holiday. But when they went back to their bunks, they found them cold and empty. The women of Health Hope were gone.

Well, hell, any port in a storm...

They went to the women of Santa Monica...

Who were also gone...

And when, at daybreak, they realized fully the horror of what had happened, a terrible picture rose up in their minds: a little man, piping a tune of sex to any woman he could find, with *now* two bands of love-starved women, following him across the world, like chains. They saw Purvis Gregory, damned forever to sleeping with every beautiful and desirable woman in the world, never stopping.

And for a long, long while, they wondered who was worse off:

Themselves...or Purvis Gregory?

Carrion Flesh

(as by "Paul Merchant")

VINCE RAGONA HAD SEEN THEM like this time and time again. The fat, round, little ones with hair clipped too short, and looking as though it were brittle; the ones with tattoos—honest to god tattoos—on their arms. Arms that were muscular and arms that were sodden with hanging fat. He had seen them like this so often he could type them in his sleep…which he did once in a while.

Franny was the madam at this crib, and he went to her first, knocking once heavily on her apartment door, and walking in uninvited.

When a man from the Syndicate comes recruiting, no freelance operator gives him any trouble, never refuses an invitation.

The room was heavily scented with *Arpège*, and Vince gagged for a moment. It brought up memories of a girl who had once used the scent, memories he had been trying to lose for a long time. He was not consciously aware of the memories, and the gagging (he thought), consequently, came from a sour stomach.

He passed the full-length mirror and caught a snap-brim reflection of himself. Tall and dark and poised, the way a Syndicate man should be. The reflection moved away, and he was in the one big easy chair Franny kept for visitors. She was nowhere in sight, but he could hear the sound of running water from the bathroom. He could imagine her in there, her legs spread as she sat in the sink, the tubes and equipment hosing out around and into and past her.

A disgusting woman, but for some reason she dragged down more clientele than any of her girls. Most crib madams didn't take in trade themselves unless it was a special occasion, but Franny was different.

She liked it, and she wanted it, and she had to keep the money coming in because every time she got a hot one in, the Syndicate stopped by to take her away, and she was left with the dogs again.

Just as it was going to happen this time.

The water died off, and Vince heard sounds of heavy breathing from the other room. The door opened with a bang, and Franny came out, a paunchy, middle-aged man with her. They were both nude, and pulled a fleecy towel between them, both dripping wet.

"C'mon, baby, gimme th' towel!" the paunchy, middle-aged man cried, laughing till tears came to his watery brown eyes.

Franny slapped him once on the chest, and dragged the towel to herself, wiping rapidly up and down her inner thighs, drying off, and starting on her hair. As she raised her eyes to massage her frowzy red hair, she saw Vince slouched in the chair, and she stopped in mid-movement.

"Blow," Vince said to the paunchy, middle-aged man.

He started to reply, drawing his ridiculous, pear-shaped body up in outrage, but Vince tossed a look at Franny. "Tell him."

Franny turned to the man, whispered something in his ear, gathered his clothes from the edge of the radiator ledge where they had been hurriedly tossed, and shoved him toward the door. He protested all the way, but she finally snapped, "No charge! No damn charge, dammit! Now get *out*!" and slammed the door on his naked behind.

She turned, draping the towel about herself carefully.

"Gimme a minute. How are ya, Vince?"

The two statements were miles apart in thought, but they came out together, as though they were somehow related and she moved to the closet door. In a moment she had taken a silk wrapper from its hanger and had it belted about herself. It was an Oriental design and the dragon lapped at the full, high pitch of her left breast.

"Two new ones. A Melody and a Gay. Get them."

She fell apart. Her face quirked into an expression of pain. "Look, Vince, they just came with me. They've only been here a week. I *need* 'em, Vince. You been draggin' off all my good girls, and these kids are fresh in the state. I *need* 'em, Vince!" Her tone had subtly shaded down to a pleading tone. She stared at him with green eyes that asked and pleaded more than the voice.

"Get 'em. I don't need to explain to you...get 'em!"

She attempted to start another sentence, broke off, and went to the door. She opened it and looked back at him.

"You bastard," she said, and the door slammed shut.

Vince smiled softly, and sat back, lighting a cigarette. He drew down on the butt, and let smoke filter out through mouth and nostrils. He watched the door silently.

There was a knock, and he said, "Come."

Two girls stood there. They looked bewildered for an instant, then realized he was in the room and they were together, and immediately drew conclusions.

"No. No tricks. Just one at a time. Come on in…you."

He motioned to the dark-haired girl with the long, long legs, and she tossed a haughty glance at the other, started to close the door.

"Wait out there," Vince said to the high-breasted blonde, and the brunette slammed the door.

The girl walked toward him, and a low whistle escaped her. "Franny told us to get in here fast, and we couldn't figure it, but you're *nice*.

"After all those lousy slugs I've tossed today, you're special, honey."

She moved toward him, her skirt swirling around her legs, and made as though to touch him.

Vince straightened back out of reach. "Knock it. Don't touch me."

Startled, she moved back a step.

Vince stared her up and down.

She was tall, and her legs were unusually long. She caught him staring and lifted her skirt, bunching it tight to her thighs. Her calves and ankles were slim in comparison with the heavy, round weight on her thighs. She wore no underpants, and the dark mat of her torso was visible. She lowered the skirt as his eyes traveled up to her flat belly, the small, pinched waist, the high, small but firm breasts, the smooth white column of her neck.

She had good features. Blue eyes and brunette hair. High cheekbones and a hungry mouth.

"Get sexy," he said, crossing his legs.

She stared at him openly for a second, trying to establish whether or not she had heard what she had heard, then she shrugged her shoulders in their peasant blouse sheath.

"Anything in particular?" she asked.

He shook his head.

She licked her lips and turned slowly, flouncing the full skirt so her calves showed white for a moment. Then she placed one hand on either side of her right leg, and slid the hands up carefully, lovingly, till she had the skirt raised above her knee. She let the fingers open till they were wrapped about her thighs, and Vince could see the darker tops of her stockings, making slight indentations against the snowy flesh of her leg. The stocking tops were rolled, and the garter buckle sank into the skin ever so slightly. She wore no underpants, but only a garter belt, and it hugged to her body tightly as a brace. A small roll of bills was stuck in the elastic of the garter belt, just touching the brunette mat of her womanliness.

She took one hand from her leg, and languorously touched one finger to her inner thigh. It was such a surprising, odd movement, it made Vince stir uneasily.

Then she grasped the hem of her skirt with both hands and brought it up, and up, and up till it was covering her lower face, and he could only see her blue eyes staring at him provocatively from above the line of cloth.

She moved then.

She rotated her hips, and let her knees come close together. She swayed first in one direction, then the other, and her body wavered ever so slightly, as her hips moved sinuously.

She let the skirt fall back abruptly, hiding the view, and unzipped the side of it. She let it fall in a whispering heap about her high-heeled feet, and stepped out of it gracefully.

Then she went to work on the blouse. With her lower half bared, she let her right hand smooth the wide neck of the blouse down her white, rounded shoulder. It pressed tightly there, drawn tighter still over her breasts, the nipples outlined even through the brassiere, through the thin cloth of the blouse. Then the other side, down, down, till it was on a line with her armpit.

She pushed the restricting blouse down her body till it was a bandeau about her waist, and her breasts were only held by the tight, black, strapless brassiere. She moved her quick, subtle hands up her stomach, clutching at the tight flesh there to show him it was not fat, pausing an instant at the navel, which she traced around its outside perimeter with her little finger. Then her hands moved on up, and pressed tightly to her breasts, flattening them.

She slid her hands around back, and he heard snaps opening. Then the brassiere dropped away, and she slid the blouse off her hips, down her legs, and stepped out of it.

Her breasts were, as he'd noted, small, but very firm. They were tip-tilted and rose with each breath she took. Their color was not sick white, but more a golden color, showing she had been sunbathing without a top. The nipples were small and cylindrical, small holes in each one showing something he was quick to let pass.

The red thin line where the brassiere had pressed in against the skin stood out against the lighter coloring of her body, and she was slightly moist as though she had been perspiring from some exertion.

He let the thought sift through his mind as to what sort of exertion she had been doing, and turned his thoughts back to the beautiful, lithe body before him.

"Now the bed," he said.

She walked to the bed and lay down, not removing her hose, only her high heels. As she slumped back on the bed her legs rose and split, in the traditional gesture of a whore's invitation. She lay there, her hands straight out, below the rounded rock of her buttocks, and her fingers moved idly, inviting him.

"Move," he said. "The way you'd do it for a customer."

She started to let her legs drop, started to protest, but he said, "Move!" angrily, and she moved.

Her hips jerked up, and she ground them sidewise against the coverlet of the bed. Her legs pressed tightly together and crossed, locking as they would behind some obstruction. She heaved up and down, swirling sidewise and arching her back. After a few moments Vince uncrossed his legs, let the cigarette now turned to ash drop to the floor.

Not looking at her he said, "Get dressed."

She dressed quickly, staring at him from time to time in bewilderment and just a trace of terror. When she was finished she walked over. "Five," she said, and he looked up suddenly.

"You don't get paid from me, humper. You just trundle you rear back into the hall and send your girlfriend in. Then wait till I call you."

She began to protest, but he let his eyes narrow down, and started to rise. She moved away quickly, and stopped at the door.

"Y'know somethin', honey," she said sweetly. "You're outta your fraykin' mind!" The she left, the door slamming closed with utter finality.

A moment later it opened again, and the blonde stood there. "Come on in, come on in," he said impatiently, "I haven't got all week."

She came in, closing the door behind her, staring around the room in wonder, questioningly.

"Gay says you're a strange one.

"Are you?"

He stared back, and his mouth split in an odd, lopsided grin. "Never can tell about anyone who patronizes a crib, can you?" he replied.

"Look, I don't go for any beating or crap like that," she said. "Odd stuff is okay as long as it's on the bed. That's what I'm paid for, but anything else I—"

"Shut up," he said.

She clamped her full lips shut, and he told her, pull up your skirt slow.

She did it carefully, her knees tight together, her feet close, and stopped at the knees. "Higher," he said. She moved the tight skirt up till it was too tight to pull any higher. She wore lacy white underpants that covered the dark path between her legs.

"Pull down your drawers," he said.

She did it, knowing now, somehow, that his orders were not to be questioned.

He ran her through the same routine, ending with her quite naked and grinding on the bed.

When she got up off her back, he said, "Come here."

She walked over to the chair, and her face was a blond mask of silence. "Sit down on my lap."

She slid onto him, and he slid lower in the chair, taking her with him. She let one silken arm go around his neck, and he put his hand down on her belly, inched it down to the edge of her torso. She gasped slightly, and her eyes closed.

He took her long blond hair in the other hand, and drew her mouth down to his. His mouth worked on hers, his tongue opening her lips, though she struggled, and he was in the moist cavern of her.

They stayed that way for a short time, then he

was businesslike again. "Up," he said.

She got off him and he ordered her to dress.

As she waited, much as the other girl had waited, he said, "Go get Franny. Tell her quick."

The girl left, and he sank back, sweating, murmuring, "Carrion flesh!"

Franny stalked in, and he said, "They'll both do. I'll come get them tomorrow."

"Look, Vince," she pleaded, "these are new girls. I need them real bad. Business has fallen way the hell off since the cops started gettin' rough, and your Syndicate started takin' a rake off. I've *got* to have these girls!"

"I ain't gonna let ya do it!" she snapped angrily.

Vince was out of the chair in an instant, his hand doubled and cracking into the stout woman's fleshy face.

"You lousy purveyor of filthy skin, you," he snapped. Yelling, he hit her again and again, till she lay on the floor, her face bloody and her wrapper torn open. He was breathing heavily, and he stood over her, legs spread.

"We've got a new house opening in Rock Creek and we want the best—considering what it is we want the best *of*—and these two make it. Now if you want to keep your crib, and keep your teeth, you better goddam well shut up."

He moved to go. Stopping at the door he tossed back, "Tomorrow. Have 'em packed and waiting."

He opened the door, took a step, she spat after him, "Lousy sluggy, stinkin' fraykin'..."

She never got the final word out, for he had turned, and his foot lashed out, catching her in the breast.

She screamed high, and slumped back, unconscious.

Vince Ragona closed the door after him, stared at the two silent girls in the hall, and moved away.

In the waiting room a darkly handsome man of twenty-eight sat, his fine, almost girlish features drawn down in an expression of distaste. His legs were crossed woman-fashioned, and his hair was perfumed.

Vince Ragona stopped before him, placed a hand on the other's knee and said softly, "Let's get out of here."

"It must be terrible for you, Vince," the first one said with a faint musical lilt to his voice.

"Paulie," Vince replied, summoning a brave smile, "a job is a job, even when it's as disgusting as this."

The effeminate one rose, and they walked to the front door together.

As they opened the door, Vince turned to Paulie, said, "Honey, you'd better be good to me tonight. I've had a rough day selecting this... this..." he fumbled, spat out, "this *carrion flesh*!"

The door closed silently.

The crib was quiet.

The Silence of Infidelity

WILLIAM: THIRTY-ONE YEARS OLD, five feet ten inches tall, weighing one hundred and seventy-seven pounds. A slight bulge just under his belt due to an affinity for pizza with pepperoni. A man who once considered elevator shoes, though he didn't really need them. A man with heartburn and a bank account of $612.08, jointly-entered in his wife's name. A thin scar that runs from his wrist to his inside elbow, which he got in his early twenties, from a threshing machine on an Iowa farm. William was happily married to

Madelaine: twenty-nine years old, five feet six inches tall, weighing just over one hundred and twelve. A woman with rich chestnut-colored hair, and friendly brown eyes. A comfortable woman, who kept a clean home, and worked part-time in a shipping concern, as a ledger recorder. A woman with definite tastes in reading matter and the type of breakfast cereal kept in the apartment. She had two children, both girls, named Roxanne and Beth, whom she treated fairly, impartially and lovingly. She had seen her husband rise from stock clerk to manager to district advisor for a group of co-operative grocery stores. She felt deep within herself that she had aided his climb by being a good wife and an understanding companion. They had been happily married for ten years.

There was a third person.

The Woman.

"We are out of ketchup, Bill," Madelaine's voice reached him in his chair before the television set. The smell of lamb chops filled the five-room apartment, and the kitchen seemed a magical country composed of nothing but delicious odor.

"Want to send Roxy down?" He asked, turning his attention from the news.

Madeline's voice was ever-so-slightly tinged with worry. "No. Bill, you mind running to the corner to get some? The neighborhood's getting pretty wild, and you just never know. We'll be eating in a few minutes...would you?"

He swung up out of the chair with a short bemused half-chuckle. "Sure, honey. Be back in five."

He didn't bother to slip on a topcoat, it was the end of October, and though the nippiness was in the air, still it was warm enough for a stroll to the Puerto Rican bodega on the corner for a bottle of ketchup.

He rang for the elevator, and lit a cigarette as he waited. If the blankness of a mind constantly thinking can be called blankness, then blank his mind was. No thoughts surged to the top, yet a vague feeling of security, of relaxation ran through him.

On the street, he walked briskly, stepping in and out of the shadows without conscious awareness of them. Yet his thoughts agreed with what Madelaine had said. The once-wealthy neighborhood *had* deteriorated. Stately apartment buildings had been cut up into single rooms and rented out to Puerto Ricans, fresh from the boats. And though he had no malice in his mind, though he did not dislike a people for its race, still they were new to American New York, and their habits were not the most sanitary.

Madelaine had been wise in not allowing Roxanne to walk these streets, even at seven o'clock.

In the bodega he said a friendly hello to the Puerto Rican owner, a drooping-moustached fellow named (inevitably) Juan. They exchanged cursory pleasantries over the counter as Juan slipped the ketchup into a bag, and accepted the coins.

William stepped out of the bodega and crossed the street against the light. Far down, at 80th Street, a stream of cars double-eyed brightly toward him, and he stepped to the other curb rapidly.

He walked up from the corner, toward his apartment building, passing the bus stop. The Woman was there, at the bus stop, waiting. He saw her as he approached, and even then his interest rose.

It was that simple, without fanfare and without preamble. She was tall, slightly taller than he, wearing black patent leather high heels that seemed a trifle higher than any he had seen before. Her legs were slim and well-formed, what he could see of them below the tweed of her skirt. The wedge of skirt that showed beneath the thigh-length leather car coat was tasteful, and matched perfectly, somehow, with the steel-grey leather car jacket. She had the collar up, and it collided with the shoulder length blond hair that fell in soft waves.

Her face was half turned away from him, and he only caught a sheer glance of uptilted nose, blue eye, and full mouth. It was, more than anything, the way she had her feet set, that made him stop.

As he passed, he looked back over his shoulder, and saw she had one foot turned outward, the way fashion models do it when they are being studiedly fashionable. He stopped, and there was something about the streetlight that cast a sheen across those few inches of nyloned legs. His eyes rose to her face; she stared at him fully.

He gripped the ketchup bottle tighter, for she didn't turn away, as a woman should, who is being stared at by a stranger on the streets. She watched him intently, and there was an arch to her well-formed eyebrows. Her eyes said something to him. William was by no means a deeply perceptive man, and he knew it, yet there was an unmistakable invitation in the Woman's eyes. His blood speeded up, and he felt a quivering in his legs. Thoughts flashed in and out of his mind like a bright fish in a clear stream.

Then the Woman smiled.

Her full, rich red mouth curved upward, and her hands, which had hung at her sides till now, rose to smooth her hips. At that movement the thought crossed William's mind that she was a prostitute.

But as her hands moved, he retracted the thought. No, not a prostitute. A Woman, yes, but not a whore.

Hardly realizing he was moving, he stepped back toward her. They stood for an instant, very close, heart's-throw close for a moment, and he saw the swell of the car jacket over her breasts. Her figure was hidden by the bulk of the steel-grey coat, yet he was certain it must be magnificently-proportioned.

He could smell the faint muskiness of her, and it filled his head with an aphrodisia that made him stagger.

As he stood next to her, staring into her symmetrical, unlined, sensuous face, she wet her lips. It was a slick, quick, razored movement that abruptly brought his mind to pictures of women lifting their skirts, showing their bodies. It was a completely sexful movement, and that pale tongue-tip slipped out and in again in an instant.

He knew then that she wanted him to come with her.

Not a word had been spoken, yet he knew what her eyes said, knew what the positioning of her feet meant, knew what that wicked little tongue had ordered in its journey.

She turned away and walked back down toward the corner, looking over her shoulder once; to let him know she was leading him. He started after her, and the thought of Madelaine and the kids and dinner scurried out of his way. He watched the fine taut line of movement as her legs scissored inside her skirt, and the pain hit him in the deepest, most remote area of his belly. The Woman was a siren; he was a helpless Argonaut. The sea was wine-dark, and he could not swim away.

She turned up the steps of the one brownstone apartment house, and he followed quickly. She opened the door with a key, and led him up three flights of stairs, to another door.

She opened this one with the same key, and reached around the inside of the jamb, flicking on the lights.

He stepped inside, and she shut the door, locking it quickly.

The apartment was tastefully furnished, without being either ultra-modern or period. It was a conglomeration of furniture, the kind of assortment a person collects having moved many times in many cities.

She took his hand then, and removed the bottle of ketchup in its brown paper bag, setting it on a table near the door. She led him to a sofa, where he sat down, unbuttoning his jacket and jerking up the creases of his pants-legs as he sat.

She walked quickly to the portable radio plugged into the wall, and turned it on. A newscaster's voice broke in. She turned the dial rapidly, bringing in a program of quiet dinner music, but the sound of the newscaster's voice had started him back along the track of the past five minutes. It had been no longer than that since he had left his apartment, left Madelaine with the lamb chops, and Roxanne spoon-feeding Beth.

Yet he didn't seem to care. He was making as big a decision as he had ever made. He was changing the course of his life, and he knew it. He was settling a barrier between himself and the life he had led with Madelaine, as surely as he sat there, yet he didn't really care.

He knew this was the way it was, *because* it was.

He did not consider the idea of sin, and he did not consider the idea of adultery. This was real, it was true, it was the way he must live, and he knew it as a certainty.

Then the Woman turned away from the radio, and unwound the belt that knotted her car coat closed. She stripped off the jacket and hung it carefully in the closet.

At that moment he wondered where she had been going, to be waiting at the bus stop, and if it could have been so unimportant an engagement that she could break it to bring him here like this, a stranger.

But he also knew, in that instant, that she had wanted *him*...not just any man, not just anybody, but *him*.

Him, pure and simple and direct and true. The way it should have been. The way it was meant to be. The way the world saw it and the way it was going to be. The way it was.

She faced him, and he was assured of her beauty. It was not a cheap or a superficial beauty. She was a handsome Woman, right through and down as deep as anyone could wish. She was not ashamed, for there was nothing to be ashamed of, and she knew what was about to happen, even as he knew.

William watched as she unbuttoned her sweater, folded it precisely on the chair beside the table. He watched with growing expectation, but without a feeling of lechery as she reached behind her and unfastened the brassiere of pink material. He stared calmly at the proud high rise of her breasts, so warm and inviting, and as she stepped close to him, signifying he should unzip her skirt, he knew this would not be the last time he would see the Woman. He knew, as his fingers touched the warm metal, that he would see her again, and whether on the subway, or on the street, or in the pharmacy, it would always end like this. That they would never say a word, and that they would never know each other's name, but that it would be just like this over and over again.

And it was right. It was the way it should be.

She slid the skirt down her hips, the silky sound of her slip rustling making the only sound over the quiet dinner music so typical of his apartment down the street.

She folded the skirt properly and laid it beside him on the sofa. She put her thumbs between the silk of her slip and the dark blue of her pants, and pulled down the half-slip. It went atop the skirt, and somehow *that* seemed so right, also.

Then the pants, and she was standing in her garter belt, stockings and shoes.

She took him by the hand and they went into the bedroom. As he watched in the filtered light from the living room, light that cast an aura around her, touching the faintly blond hairs that covered her body like down, she turned down the covers on the single bed.

Then she sat on the bed and unfastened her garters, stripped down her stockings, removed her shoes, and took off the nylon hose. Then she took off the garter belt, and lay on the bed, perfectly flat: a great painting of exquisite gentleness. Finally, she raised her lower body so she could slip out of the dark blue panties. Then she lay back on the bed, perfectly flat again.

Then her legs parted, and a minute later received him.

Afterward, she went into the bathroom and locked the door. He knew what she meant. That it was through for this time, and that she wanted no money, that she had done it because she had done it, and there were no recriminations, no apologies, nothing to be said. It was done, and she had wanted him as William, with a false plate, and with heartburn, and with a bank balance of $612.08 jointly in his wife's name.

He dressed quickly and left the apartment, not even taking notice of the number on the door. He would know it when he came again, for he would not come alone. He would be led by her, and he would never come there unless she *did* lead him; that was the silent bargain they had made.

He knew every line of her body, as well as he had grown to know Madelaine's in the ten years of their marriage. He knew the feel of her hair and the scent of her body. He knew where every bit of furniture stood.

He walked out onto the street, and the air had turned chillier. Yet he walked slowly, feeling the sting of the air as he drew it into his lungs.

There had been nothing said, yet the message was there for always.

He opened his apartment door with his key and walked in. Madelaine hurried out of the kitchen at the sound of the closing door and stared at him oddly, hands on her hips, eyes sparkling.

"Bill, where *were* you? I've already eaten, and Roxanne, too. We went ahead. The chops are cold. I'll have to heat them for you now. We ate them without ketchup. Where were you?"

William handed her the bottle of ketchup in its brown paper bag, and kissed her lightly on the cheek.

His mind was quiet, and there was a feeling of fulfillment that mounted to his chest as he said, "I met an old, old friend. We had a few things to say to one another."

And he did not lie.

IF YOU MISSED IT, GO BACK AND BUY THE FIRST BOOK: "PULLING A TRAIN" IT'S ONLY MAGNIFICENT!

CHRONOLOGY
OF BOOKS BY
HARLAN ELLISON
1958-2012

NOVELS:

WEB OF THE CITY [1958]

THE SOUND OF A SCYTHE [1960] [2011]

SPIDER KISS [1961]

SHORT NOVELS:

DOOMSMAN [1967]

ALL THE LIES THAT ARE MY LIFE [1980]

RUN FOR THE STARS [1991]

MEFISTO IN ONYX [1993]

SHORT STORY COLLECTIONS:

THE DEADLY STREETS [1958]

SEX GANG (as by "Paul Merchant") [1959]

A TOUCH OF INFINITY [1960]

CHILDREN OF THE STREETS [1961]

GENTLEMAN JUNKIE and Other Stories of the Hung-Up
Generation [1961]

ELLISON WONDERLAND [1962]

PAINGOD and Other Delusions [1965]

I HAVE NO MOUTH & I MUST SCREAM [1967]

FROM THE LAND OF FEAR [1967]

LOVE AIN'T NOTHING BUT SEX MISSPELLED [1968]

THE BEAST THAT SHOUTED LOVE AT THE HEART OF
THE WORLD [1969]

OVER THE EDGE [1970]

ALL THE SOUNDS OF FEAR
(British publication only) [1973]

DE HELDEN VAN DE HIGHWAY
(Dutch publication only) [1973]

APPROACHING OBLIVION [1974]

THE TIME OF THE EYE (British publication only) [1974]

DEATHBIRD STORIES [1975]

NO DOORS, NO WINDOWS [1975]

HOE KAN IK SCHREEUWEN ZONDER MOND
(Dutch publication only) [1977]

STRANGE WINE [1978/2004]

SHATTERDAY [1980]

STALKING THE NIGHTMARE [1982]

ANGRY CANDY [1988]

ENSAMVÄRK (Swedish publication only) [1992]

JOKES WITHOUT PUNCHLINES [1995]

BCE 3BYKN CTPAXA (ALL FEARFUL SOUNDS)
(Unauthorized Russian publication only) [1997]

THE WORLDS OF HARLAN ELLISON (Authorized
Russian publication only) [1997]

SLIPPAGE [1997]

*KOLETIS, KES KUULUTAS ARMASTUST MAAILMA
SÜDAMES* (Estonian publication only) [1999]

LA MACHINE AUX YEUX BLEUS (French publication
only) [2001]

TROUBLEMAKERS [2001]

PTAK SMIERCI (THE BEST OF HARLAN ELLISON)
(Polish publication only) [2003]

DEATHBIRD STORIES (Expanded edition) [2011]

PULLING A TRAIN [2012]

GETTING IN THE WIND [2012]

OMNIBUS VOLUMES:

FANTASIES OF HARLAN ELLISON [1979]

DREAMS WITH SHARP TEETH [1991]

COLLABORATIONS:

PARTNERS IN WONDER: Collaborations with
14 Other Wild Talents [1971]

THE STARLOST: PHOENIX WITHOUT ASHES
(With Edward Bryant) [1975]

MIND FIELDS: 33 STORIES INSPIRED BY
THE ART OF JACEK YERKA [1994]

I HAVE NO MOUTH, AND I MUST SCREAM:
The Interactive CD-Rom (Co-Designed with
David Mullich and David Sears) [1995]

"REPENT, HARLIQUIN!" SAID THE TICKTOCKMAN
(Rendered paintings by Rick Berry) [1997]

2000X (Host and Creative Consultant of National Public
Radio episode series) [2000-2001]

GRAPHIC NOVELS:

DEMON WITH A GLASS HAND (adaptation with
Marshall Rogers) [1986]

NIGHT AND THE ENEMY (adaptation with Ken Steacy)
[1987]

VIC AND BLOOD: THE CHRONICLES OF A BOY AND
HIS DOG (adaptation with Richard Corben) [1989]

HARLAN ELLISON'S DREAM CORRIDOR,
Volume One [1996]

VIC AND BLOOD: THE CONTINUING ADVENTURES
OF A BOY AND HIS DOG (adaptation with
Richard Corben) [2003]

HARLAN ELLISON'S DREAM CORRIDOR,
Volume Two [2007]

PHOENIX WITHOUT ASHES (art by Alan Robinson
and John K. Snyder III) [2010/2011]

NON-FICTION & ESSAYS:

MEMOS FROM PURGATORY [1961]

THE GLASS TEAT: *Essays of Opinion on Television* [1970]

THE OTHER GLASS TEAT: *Further Essays of Opinion
on Television* [1975]

THE BOOK OF ELLISON (edited by Andrew Porter)
[1978]

SLEEPLESS NIGHTS IN THE PROCRUSTEAN BED
(edited by Marty Clark) [1984]

AN EDGE IN MY VOICE [1985]

HARLAN ELLISON'S WATCHING [1989]

THE HARLAN ELLISON HORNBOOK [1990]

BUGF#CK! The Useless Wit & Wisdom of Harlan Ellison
(edited by Arnie Fenner) [2011]

SCREENPLAYS & SUCHLIKE:

THE ILLUSTRATED HARLAN ELLISON (edited by
Byron Preiss) [1978]

HARLAN ELLISON'S MOVIE [1990]

I, ROBOT: THE ILLUSTRATED SCREENPLAY (based
on Isaac Asimov's story-cycle) [1994]

THE CITY ON THE EDGE OF FOREVER [1996]

RETROSPECTIVES:

ALONE AGAINST TOMORROW: A 10-year Survey [1971]

THE ESSENTIAL ELLISON: *A 35-year Retrospective*
(edited by Terry Dowling, with Richard Delap &
Gil Lamont) [1987]

THE ESSENTIAL ELLISON: *A 50-year Retrospective*
(edited by Terry Dowling) [2001]

UNREPENTANT: *A Celebration of the Writing of Harlan
Ellison* (edited by Robert T. Garcia) [2010]

AS EDITOR:

DANGEROUS VISIONS [1967]

NIGHTSHADE & DAMNATIONS: *The Finest Stories
of Gerald Kersh* [1968]

AGAIN, DANGEROUS VISIONS [1972]

MEDEA: HARLAN'S WORLD [1985]

DANGEROUS VISIONS (the 35th anniversary edition)
[2002]

JACQUES FUTRELLE'S "THE THINKING MACHINE"
STORIES [2003]

THE HARLAN DISCOVERY SERIES:

STORMTRACK by James Sutherland [1975]

AUTUMN ANGELS by Arthur Byron Cover [1975]

THE LIGHT AT THE END OF THE UNIVERSE by
Terry Carr [1976]

ISLANDS by Marta Randall [1976]

INVOLUTION OCEAN by Bruce Sterling [1978]

THE WHITE WOLF SERIES:

EDGEWORKS 1: OVER THE EDGE & AN EDGE IN
MY VOICE [1996]

EDGEWORKS 2: SPIDER KISS & STALKING THE
NIGHTMARE [1996]

EDGEWORKS 3: THE HARLAN ELLISON HORNBOOK
& HARLAN ELLISON'S MOVIE [1997]

EDGEWORKS 4: LOVE AIN'T NOTHING BUT SEX
MISSPELLED & THE BEAST THAT SHOUTED LOVE AT
THE HEART OF THE WORLD [1997]

EDGEWORKS ABBEY OFFERINGS:
(IN ASSOCIATION WITH PUBLISHING 180):

BRAIN MOVIES: THE ORIGINAL TELEPLAYS OF
HARLAN ELLISON (Volume One) [2011]

BRAIN MOVIES: THE ORIGINAL TELEPLAYS OF
HARLAN ELLISON (Volume Two) [2011]

HARLAN 101: ENCOUNTERING ELLISON [2011]

HARLAN 101: THE SOUND OF A SCYTHE AND 3
CLASSIC NOVELLAS [2011]

MOTION PICTURE (DOCUMENTARY):

DREAMS WITH SHARP TEETH (A Film About Harlan
Ellison produced and directed by Erik Nelson) [2009]

AUDIO COLLECTIONS READ BY THE AUTHOR:

ON THE ROAD WITH HARLAN ELLISON (Volume One)
[1983/2001]

THE VOICE FROM THE EDGE: I HAVE NO MOUTH,
AND I MUST SCREAM (Volume One) [2002]

THE VOICE FROM THE EDGE: MIDNIGHT IN THE
SUNKEN CATHEDRAL (Volume Two) [2001]

ON THE ROAD WITH HARLAN ELLISON
(Volume Two) [2004]

RUN FOR THE STARS [2005]

ON THE ROAD WITH HARLAN ELLISON
(Volume Three) [2007]

THE VOICE FROM THE EDGE: PRETTY MAGGIE
MONEYEYES (Volume Three) [2009]

ON THE ROAD WITH HARLAN ELLISON (Volume
Four) [2010]

ON THE ROAD WITH HARLAN ELLISON: HIS LAST
BIG CON (Volume Five) [2011]

ON THE ROAD WITH HARLAN ELLISON: THE GRAND
MASTER COLLECTION (Volume Six) [2012]

THE VOICE FROM THE EDGE: DEATHBIRD
AND OTHER STORIES (Volume 4) [2011]

THE VOICE FROM THE EDGE: SHATTERDAY
AND OTHER STORIES (Volume 5) [2011]

NECESSARY

WHILE THEY LAST

**Alluring scents for women and men.
Generous 1/2 ounce perfume in exquisite
glass vial with presentation box.**

SIN TIME (GETTING IN THE WIND) Venial vixens
will find that this exotic elixer evokes excitement at any
hour of the day or nite. This big girl scent is equally
magnetic for big boys. A pair of tiny dice inside the bottle
add a dash to the splash.

GARBAGE (LORD OF GARBAGE) The brooding
complexity of Kim Fowley's signature scent is reflected
in this fruity but absurd potion that suits lads and
ladies alike. Sprinkle on a pillow before sleep, and all will
become evident. Packaged with authentic shredded
KF garbage.

Send All Orders to KICKS BOOKS CO.,

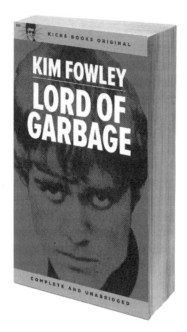